The Mephistophelean House

Benjamin Robert Carrico

Book and cover design by
Benjamin Robert Carrico

ISBN-10: 0990550710
ISBN-13: 978-0-9905507-1-6

Available in paperback, eBook, and audiobook.

www.mephistopheleanhouse.com

Chapters

For the House

1 · The Mephistophelean House

Freezing rain fell.
The snow was like glass.
"Where should we look?"
"Hawthorne?"
Matthew white-knuckled the wheel.
"We won't find anything."
"It's worth a try."
The engine pinged.
"Fuel's starting to gel. Better pull over."
The Buckthorns on Taylor were gnarly and bare. The snowmen were covered in ice. The engine cut out and we rolled to a stop. Matthew turned off the headlights.
"Here's a good place as any."
"All right. Let's go."
"What's that?"
Matthew pointed to a wheel on the corner.
"Let's take a look."
A cynosure fixed to the base of the wheel bore the colophon mark of an epigraph seal. A mirror was set in the stone tile below. I got on my knees to brush off the wet snow. Mouth. Eyes. Ear. Hair. The pieces held up. But the whole wasn't there.
"Want to spin?"
"No thanks. I believe in free will."
I spun the wheel. I was desperate. A fire gutted the

second story of my apartment building. The landlord was arrested for arson. My roommate, Geoff Jonsrud, moved to Sublimity. Weeks of looking for an affordable place in inner-southeast Portland resulted in desperation. I combed craigslist for apartments, rooms, and sub-lets, finding Matthew in similar straits. I didn't know anything about him. He didn't know anything about me.

We were complete strangers.

"What do you do, anyway?" I asked.

"I'm between jobs."

"Is that why you're moving?"

"My roommates had a…falling out."

"Oh?"

"Borderline personality disorder. Never look a gift horse in the mouth."

"Borderline personality disorder?"

"There is no such thing as coincidence, Ben. Everything happens for a reason."

"I thought you said you believed in free will."

"You're a smart guy."

Matthew patted my shoulder.

"What happened?"

"Things got out of hand."

"Really?"

"In one ear and out the other. I couldn't get a word in edgewise."

The wheel rasped in the snow.

The colophon pointed to a tree in a forest of sand.

It read, "The Weeping Tree."

"The Weeping Tree."

We left the bio diesel in a row of parked cars. Portland was a ghost town. Hawthorne was a museum of taverns, jewelers, sword mongers, psychics, saloons, tattooists, boutiques, chocolatiers, tea houses and head shops. From Colonial Heights to Sunnyside's mid-city mansions, matchbox condos, Craftsmans, bungalows, and duplexes, there were no 'For Rent' signs.

It was snowing so hard I could barely see.

"Nothing."

"Not a single sign."

"I can't believe it."

The transformer hummed, snowflakes pouring like salt from a shaker. I shivered maniacally, brushing the snow from my eyes.

Matthew chattered.

"Let's go back."

I stared at the warmly lit, advent-calendar-like windows.

"What made us think we could just go out and find a place? We don't have a lot of money and we don't know anybody. We'd have better luck in Felony Flats."

"I'm not going back," I said.

"What do you suggest?"

"Let's call it quits."

We trudged back to the car. Half an inch of freezing rain had accumulated on the bio diesel. Matthew tugged the handle. The door remained fast.

"Frozen."

I wrenched the door ajar. We got in. Matthew throttled the motor.

"I don't know what made us think we could find a place. Hawthorne and Belmont are like Height and Ashbury, Babylon and Bohemia rolled into one sales-taxless post-capitalist bacchanalian haven."

I sank back in the cold leather seat.

"We'd be better off looking somewhere else."

The cabin warmed, thawing the ice that accompanied my misery.

"Try driving up Hawthorne."

"We can't afford anything on Mount Tabor."

"Do you have a better idea?"

Ice needles, frost flowers, agates and crowns, branch collars gilded and heavy, fissures that ran through the ice-meddled jamb, houses that were dark and empty. A barbican stood at the top of the hill barely visible in the algific aril, a sepia lighthouse's lantern room glow disappeared into the gusting down-pouring snow.

"What's that?"

I pointed up Hawthorne.

"That's the old asylum."

"Asylum?"

"Hawthorne used to be called Asylum Road."

"Look. A sign."

Nailed to a pole on the side of the road was a 'For Rent' sign.

Matthew pulled over.

"It can't be. $1200 a month for that?"

A triplex with flagstone siding was buried in the snow. Matthew squinted.

"No. Look. 1331 NE 45th. It's North."

Matthew plugged the number into his phone.

"No answer."

"Try again."

Matthew redialed.

"No luck."

"What do we do?"

"Let's take a look."

"Why? Chances are someone's already taken it."

"Nah. They would have taken down the sign."

"What if we can't get a hold of the owner?"

"No harm in looking."

The bio diesel plowed 45th, counting down the 1300 block.

"We're almost there. It's on this block."

"Look at the numbers. We've gone too far. We missed it."

"How could we have missed it?"

An old church stood on the corner of 45th and Main. A cracked staircase led through some Hawthorn trees, a low garden wall, an easement, and an empty lot.

"There's nothing here," Matthew said.

"1331 SE 45th. It's got to be here."

"Look for yourself."

We got out.

"I wonder what's through those trees."

Matthew cut through the easement.

"Ben! Take a look at this."

"What?"

"I was right. There is a 1331."

The Mephistophelean House, like any other house, was the sort of place you might miss driving by, nondescript, unremarkable, indistinguishable from the all the other houses on the block, the Mephistophelean House was a House you'd find in any neighborhood, in any town, a House you'd remember a couple doors down, a place you thought you'd recognize, although you'd never been inside. Set back from the street in a ring of Hawthorns, the power line from the transformer was torn.

"A tree fell on the line."

We stood in the yard looking up at the Mephistophelean House, dormers pitch-black, eaves raked in frost, windows like a house in a dream. Chutes of ice sluiced a sill on the frieze, colorless icicles hung from the trees. The feeling of strangeness then slowly increased as we stood on the porch in a pile of debris. The living room fixtures were plated in brass, each with at least twenty five panes of glass. A balustered staircase across the front hall had a wainscot which ran the whole length of the wall.

"Looks abandoned."

"I can't believe it's only $1200. Look at the size of it! Who knows how many rooms it has?"

"I don't like it."

"What's not to like?"

"Strange how these houses look similar."

"It's a Craftsman. They built them from kits."

I stood on the porch looking up at the Mephistophelean House.

"It's no good. The numbers disconnected."

"Maybe you wrote the wrong number."

"I remember the number."

"Wait a minute. We're in luck. Somebody's home."

"What?"

"They see us. They're coming to the door."

The Hawthorns unloosed a crystalline diaspora.

The front door opened.

"Hell...hello…"

There was no one there.

"Matthew, there's no…."

"Storm's knocked the power out, title's in escrow. Come back another day, House isn't ready to show."

The outline of a hulking figure stood in the hall.

"See," I said, "power's out. Better come back later."

"It's now or never. Wait and it'll be gone," Matthew cleared his throat. "We'd like to see the place now, if you'd be willing to show us."

"I'll show you if you see what you came to see."

"Yes."

"Are you kidding?"

"What have we got to lose?"

"Free will," I joked.

"I don't believe in free will."

A phantasmal snow fell. I braced against the cold, not wanting to go in, not wanting to wait outside, but Matthew entered and I was forced to follow, the glow from the lamp fading on the hardwood floor. The Mephistophelean House was larger than it appeared, bleak and cheerless, with white walls and mahogany wainscoting, tapered square columns, and handcrafted mixed material woodwork.

An inordinate amount of keys jangled on a ring.

"That's a lot of keys," I said.

"There are a lot of doors that need locking," came the reply.

"Are you the landlord," Matthew asked.

"Something like that."

"My name's Matthew. This is Ben. And you are?"

"Ogemtel."

"Thank you for showing us the place, Mr. Ogemtel."

Blood-tertiary hardwoods rose-hipped cabinets of cherry and glass, 10ft ceilings and pocket doors, a dumbwaiter, scullery and kitchen. At times it seemed the jangling keys weren't there, and Matthew and I were alone.

"I don't like this," I said.

"It's an old House, 100 years old, 100 years old this year. It's well made of Craftsman's trade, the timbers are well sewn, old growth beams from old tall trees cut down and interwoven. A House, a hill, a basement still, a Home for you two boys. A palace for a pauper's price. Don't worry about the noise."

"I don't know what kind of references you need from us Mr. Ogemtel," Matthew interrupted, "but as far as we're concerned, we love the place and we want to move in. We brought a certified check, right Ben?"

"Sometimes they get out."

"Can you do a credit check here or is it going to take a couple of hours? What are the lease terms, by the way? Would we have the option of an additional year?"

"They?"

"The people."

"People?"

"In the House on the Hill."

"Will it be first and last plus deposit or just first and last? Is there a cleaning fee? I can't help noticing the place smells like cats. Are there other people? What are our chances, because I'm ready to sign a lease today. Hmm, Ben?"

"We build a wall to keep them in, but sometimes they get out, and look for small forgotten holes when cracks begin to sprout. Brick by brick we pick the sick, and guard them night and day, but no matter how tall we build the wall, there's always another one getting away. So up we build, a wall instilled, buttressed in steel and thorns, and warn the ones left locked inside a curse which it adorns, but even if our walls were built so high they'd touch the sky, there would always be by chance the one to teach himself to fly."

I reached out.

There was nothing there.

"You don't have to worry, though, about them that get out. Violently deranged they are, and tend to roam about. You needn't bother to refrain, nor pay them any clout, for here is one set back old House they'd rather do without. As solid as sarcophagi, these walls a secret holds, stay awhile, you might find out, a mystery unfolds."

2 · Moving In

The Gorge wind masticated the Avenue of the Roses like a Gatling gun on an ice shelf. Rocky Butte was curtained in snow. A bourbon pickup pulled into the parking lot of Terrace Grove Apartments, Geoff Jonsrud's straight pipe belching like a devil's fork. I stamped my boots on the Jersey wall, drinking a cup of coffee.

"So what do you think?" Jonsrud fished in his pockets for a lighter.

"I don't have any options," I said.

"What's wrong?"

"What isn't?"

"Better than this dump."

"I'm not so sure."

"How'd you see it in the dark?"

"There wasn't much to see."

"Sounds too good to be true."

The Avenue of the Roses was a path of least resistance through the Boring Lava Field. New wood drooped over static wires. Gravel pitted the snow dump. I drank my coffee while Jonsrud smoked. Snow blew across the road.

"I guess this is it."

"Yep."

Jonsrud stamped his cigarette on the veneer.

"Let's go."

We emptied the apartment in four trips.

I took one last look around.

"I'm gonna miss this place."

"We had some good times here."

"We had some good times. Not here."

Matthew shivered in the yard of a blue, three-story house on South Tabor. We parked in the driveway. Matthew introduced himself to Jonsrud and got in the cab.

"Isn't he going to help?"

"I guess he's expecting us to do it."

We loaded the bed. I lost my balance and fell. Jonsrud helped me up, reattaching the mount.

Matthew never looked up.

Most of the shops on Hawthorne were closed. We turned onto 45th, the narrow, snow chocked intersection adjacent the woodworker, the cracked staircase, the Hawthorn trees, the low garden wall.

"Where is it?"

"Through there."

Jonsrud parked. We cut through the easement. The Mephistophelean House poked through the Hawthorns.

The landlord was not on the porch.

"Are we early?"

"We're late."

Matthew tried the front door.

"It's open."

"No one's here."

"Keys are in the hall."

"Here's a copy of the lease."

"What does it say?"

"Just our names are on it."

"That's odd."

A heavy layer of dust permeated the Mephistophelean House, a wall of dead air dulling the perception of time and space. I unlatched the rod and opened the window, an immaculate floe dispelling the emptiness that filled the room.

"Stuffy."

"Like a crowded room."

"But we're the only ones here."

Jonsrud and I hoisted the box springs, mattresses, and furniture upstairs, leaving the boxes unpacked.

Matthew disappeared upstairs.

"Where is he?"

"Choosing his room, I'm sure."

"Didn't bring anything up."

"Didn't load anything, either."

Ripples, waves and indentations warped the window panes, the Hawthorn trees excoriated in the freezing rain. The kitchen had a coffered ceiling, windowed nook and grill, a zinc and brass utensil rack, a marble peppermill.

"I'd better get rolling," Jonsrud said.

"What? Don't you want to get some pizza?"

"Nah. Better hit the road."

We said our goodbyes.

The front door closed.

Matthew appeared.

"I'll take the room by the stairs. It's got a sleeping porch."

"Sleeping porch?" I asked.

"It's got windows at both ends."

"Oh."

"You're an early riser, right?"

"No..."

"Then you'll enjoy the room at the end of the hall."

"Want some help with your boxes?"

"Brrr. Drafty old house. We'll have to keep the heat on at all times."

Matthew turned the thermostat to maximum.

"Thanks for your help."

Snow spilled through the open window. The furnace rumbled. I closed the window and turned down the thermostat.

The kitchen floor was scuffed and marked, a cooker missing its handle, the rusted cart of a dumbwaiter shaft, a box of old paraffin candles. Out of place the basement door was freshly painted white. I unlocked the bolt and used my hand to find the basement light. A hose and pump whirred in a trough that ran along the floor. A dowel and a door frame leaned against a chest of drawers. A jib door with a lock rail opened underneath the flue, the casing barely wide enough for someone to fit through.

"Hmmm. Wonder what's inside."

There were no windows.

I hesitated, wondering what was beyond the narrow sphere of light. Water spilled under the door. From the vent came the buzzing of flies.

The pump at the base of the staircase discharged.

The furnace racketed like a meat grinder.

Matthew unpacked in a room at the top of the stairs. Tall and bright with hardwood floors and closets at both ends, the windows towered through the trees that looked out on the hills.

"Your room's down the hall."

Across the hall was a grim little room with a curious double-hung window. The window looked out on a Walnut tree growing between the old hip and the awning. An abnormal closet, a false little room, with a trap door, marks on the ceiling, an abrasion or stain I couldn't explain made the room even more unappealing.

"What's that smell?"

I got the vacuum from downstairs and cleaned the grim white room. To embed the hose head underneath the baseboard I reworked the crack back and forth under the floor.

"The place smells like cats."

"There's something under the floor."

"What the hell is it?"

"I don't know."

The baseboard was bilgy.

"I wonder how long it's been empty."

"A long time, by the looks of it."

I rolled the vacuum down the hall, an inch of dust was on the wall, the hardwood, ceiling, windowsills were pocketed in cobwebbed filth. I got a bucket and some rags and opened up a garbage bag. The broom kicked up a frowsy din, the bucket instantly blackened, the grim white room ranked fell and stale, the walls were pinned in human nails.

Matthew sat on a mat.

"What are you doing?"

"Yoga."

"This place is disgusting."

"I'll smudge."

Matthew lit a stick of yarrow and set it on an altar.

"What's that gonna to do?"

"I'm announcing my presence."

"Announcing your presence?"

"And asking unwanted guests to kindly depart."

"Aren't you going to clean?"

Matthew pointed at the burning yarrow.

"Look."

The smoke was weird.

I refilled the bucket and returned to the grim little room, working methodically until dark. I got my sleeping bag and lay in bed. I must have fallen asleep for I was awakened by gurgling raucous enough to wake the dead.

I opened my eyes.

It was morning.

Snow was falling.

I looked out the window.

The pigeons were in the Walnut tree.

The trap door was open.

Something was coming down.

The pigeons flew away.

The trap door dripped on the floor, black marking a sign of wear, not a stain or mold as I had originally thought. The grim little room narrowed and I found myself going downstairs. The white door was open. Barefoot on the basement floor a stranger to myself I saw the melting snow begin to bleed and change to something else, etching icy picric fingers round the very spot I stood, while I tried to move my body but my efforts did no good. A sparking cord plugged in the line was floating in the cement through, the crushing weight then left my chest and I began to hack and cough, so I jumped and grabbed the iron railing, swinging up across and bounded up the basement staircase through the black mold and the rot.

Matthew poked his head in the kitchen.

"What's up?"

"The trap door's open."

"What?"

We went upstairs.

The trap door was nailed shut.

"It was open."

"Let's find out where it leads."

The hallway led to Matthew's room.

"There's nothing here."

"Let's check the sleeping porch."

The sleeping porch was empty.

"There's no other exit."

"What about the dumbwaiter?"

"The apparatus is gone."

"That's not all."

"What else?"

"I thought I was sleepwalking. I went downstairs. Water spilled over the floor. I nearly electrocuted myself."

"What? Are you serious?"

"See for yourself."

We went downstairs.

"Look."

I pointed at the basement floor.

"Hmm," Matthew scratched his head. "When did this happen?"

"Just now."

"The floor is level. You say you came down here for no reason?"

"I thought I was sleepwalking."

Spurs and leaders formed a minatory crown.

The pattern was unmistakable.

It was the Weeping Tree.

We went upstairs.

Matthew went to the scullery and got a head of kale. He set a Santoku on a cutting board and opened a bag of vegetables.

"I wonder what's in that room."

"What room?"

"The room by the flue."

"I didn't see any room."

"There's a door. Come on, I'll show you."

"I wouldn't be caught dead down there."

"What?"

"The stench is overpowering. Who knows what fungi, mold, rayon, natural gas cocktail we just breathed in? I wouldn't go back down there if you paid me."

"What about the trap door?"

"You saw it. It was nailed shut."

"But, I…"

Matthew unpacked a steamer and plugged it in.

"What are you making?"

"Kale, wheat grass, and beets."

"Sounds good."

I opened the refrigerator and got a package of bacon.

Matthew sneered.

"You know Ben, you are what you eat."

I clenched my teeth.

"I disagree. I think in America one is judged not by what one eats, but by the content of their character."

"Ha, ha. Very democratic," Matthew was noisome, "well, you know, I'm sure, that processed meat is bad for you."

"Really?"

"Processed meat will be the death of you."

Matthew brandished a liberal dose of honey.

"By the way, I'm going to the hardware store today to get some, er, supplies."

"Supplies?"

"Er, yeah…"

"Er yeah what?"

"Supplies for the…drainage pools."

"What drainage pools?"

"Two simple words, Ben. Carbon Neutral."

"Where are you going with this?"

"Ever given Personal Recycling a thought Ben?"

I shuddered.

"Personal Recycling?"

"Ben?"

"Yes?"

"Be honest. Do you recycle?"

"You mean paper and bottles?"

"I'm talking about carbon emissions, Ben. World carbon emissions. I'm talking about your Personal Carbon Profile."

"Personal Carbon Profile?"

"I'm talking about the Carbon Cycle, Ben. I'm talking about counting your Carbs. The Carbs that count. Your personal waste."

Matthew looked down.

"That's exactly what I mean, Ben." Matthew rested a clammy hand on my shoulder. "Where does all that 'crap' go? Hmmmm? Ben? Where does it go?"

"It goes in the toilet."

Matthew laughed.

"A simple answer to a complex question. Where does it go when you flush it down the toilet? Where does it end up?"

"I don't know, Matthew."

"Does anyone know?"

"I guess not."

"No one cares until the crap hits the fan, hmm Ben? It's the same sad story, told over and over again, history doomed to repeat itself throughout history. But instead of being a slave to history, why not be its master? Why not give a crap? Before it's too late?"

"What do you expect me to do about it?"

"Count your Carbs."

"Living things are made of carbon, Matthew. There's no way around it. Scientists believe life in other galaxies may theoretically be based on other elements, but we're not in other galaxies, are we Matthew? We're stuck here. And here, Mathew, life is Carbon. Carbon is life. They're inseparable."

"It's about Carbon Consciousness, Ben."

The arm came again.

"Personal Recycling."

I looked up at Matthew.

I neither affirmed, nor disaffirmed him.

In a way, I hated him.

"Do you want to personally recycle?"

"I'll think about it."

"Before things are said and done Ben, I bet I'll have you recycling on a personal basis."

Matthew coughed in my face.

"I think I'm coming down with something. I tossed and turned all night. Every time I shut my eyes I had the same nightmare."

"Really?" I wiped my face.

"There was an immense metal ball, as large as the universe, devouring everything in its path, and I realized how fast I'd have to go, just to stay ahead."

Matthew threw his dishes in the sink and drove off.

I worked all morning, scrubbing and cleaning the bathroom, hall, and staircase. Years of neglect and disuse had taken their toll on a House that had seen better days. It was the kind of House that was no longer built because the world had changed. The low pitched roof line, decorative brackets, exposed rafters and overhanging eaves, the timber razed from climax forests where towns had grown in their place. The Mephistophelean House was a prize, an American bungalow, but as I worked I felt uneasy. I did not like being alone.

I stopped at noon for lunch. A sandwich stand on 44th and Hawthorne was open. The cook rubbed his hands for warmth listening to a podcast of Wait Wait Don't Tell Me. Sub-freezing temperatures hardened a slippery veneer over the snowpack. I hurried back in the unrelenting wind, the old church despoiled in ice.

"Hmm. Guess no one's going to church today."

I ate my sandwich in the kitchen. The rosemary bun was buttered and toasted, the Rockfish peppered and lemony. I wadded the grease paper into the trash and dipped my wrinkled hands into another bucket. Cobwebs covered the wainscoting so I swept the black iron grills, bench, and windowsills before mopping the hall, living and dining room. When I opened the cupboard gnats swarmed like pepper-black lentigines. The bathroom was equally vile, a broken toilet leaking into the subfloor.

I worked until dark, rolling the trash out onto the parking strip. Flurries licked rooftops clean of glistening sheens of freezing rain. I returned to the kitchen and got a brown paper sack.

All that remained was the basement.

The light bulb swayed over the basement landing. The pattern was no longer visible. I set the sack on the floor and unplugged the power cord, placing a fan at the base of the stairs. I reset the pump, checked the hose, and began to sweep the floor.

The broom caught the door under the flue.

"Idiot. Door's right here."

I swept, keeping an eye on the door.

"Damned House is falling apart."

The floor was caked. I got a can of aerosol baking soda and powdered the drywall. Mold dissolved into gray bands, the deteriorated foundation a moldy plunge pool of agar and soot. I set the can down and wiped my hands. The Mephistophelean House was finished except for one place.

The door under the flue was moldered in cobwebs.

I palmed the knob.

"Hello?"

The inner, windowless chamber was utterly dark.

I opened the circuit panel. All the circuits were on, except #16 and #17. I flicked #16. Nothing happened. I tried again. The switch had no effect.

"Hmmm. Must be something upstairs."

I flicked #17. A light bulb hung on a wire inside the windowless chamber. It was dark so I pulled a box of light bulbs from the sack and found a socket on a line.

The bulb didn't light.

I tried another.

It was no good.

It was impenetrably dim. A second iron line ran parallel the first. I snatched another bulb from the box but it rang dead. I fit a third bulb in the socket, but it did not light.

The cinderblock fell over.

I looked behind my shoulder.

There was something on the line.

I fumbled another bulb, but it, like the others, did not light. The single working bulb distorted the dimensions of the room. I glanced one final socket, desperate it was true and the line had power.

The element caught.

It was as bright as day.

The windowless chamber was pockmarked in marl and gley. Double ringed upside-down stars paralleled symbols, numbers and bars under a bursiform black letter X and a bright freshly painted pink circle.

"X marks the spot."

A third bulb illuminated the windowless chamber. It was long and fell. The air was full of cinders. I went over and inspected the items on a shelf, god's pennies, a holy water sprinkler, a porcelain angel. The porcelain angel was missing its eyes.

The dumbwaiter was empty. Rungs of a ladder led up the dark shaft.

"I was right. There is a way up to the attic."

For a flooded basement, the windowless chamber was exceptionally wired. I wondered what it had been used for, what the upside-down numbers meant. The foamy pink circle was a void star. The black X was a field of scalars. As I pondered the black X and pink circle I hardly noticed the light bulbs fading, thinking perhaps there had been something there, hanging on the wall, something you couldn't take your eyes off, and though the light bulbs muddied, giving off the light of two, then one, then hardly any light at all, I gazed into the black X and pink circle, the wall overlapping, lights out, the black X and pink circle one continuous, nonterminating figure.

I stood in the windowless chamber though it would have been difficult to call myself me.

There was a red. oblong box.

Inside was a mirror.

When I looked in the mirror, I saw something I wasn't supposed to see.

3 · The Sickness

It snowed overnight. I walked to Hollywood in the dark. The ticket machine was broken so I waited on the platform without a ticket. The MAX pulled into the station and the doors opened.

There was nowhere to sit.

"The doors are closing."

I squeezed onboard. The MAX traversed Sullivan's Gulch and the Steel Bridge before rocketing into the Goose Hollow tunnel. A faded sun burned meekly, the west hills were blanketed in white, and I forgot all about the windowless chamber and the Mephistophelean House.

I took the four o'clock train back to the city. Pioneer Square was picturesque, white lights and bay laurel, peppermint candles, holly wreaths and menorahs, the Cinnamon Bear, a holiday bazaar with super track monorail, reign deer, elves and a tree.

"I think I'll stop by Peacock Lane."

Skiers mushed over the Hollywood overpass. A boy dragged his brother on a sled. Cars queued up Stark. Peacock Lane was ethereal, electric candy canes, mangers, reindeer, and elves, babies in hats and mittens, carolers, black labs, nativity scenes, Rudolphs and green plywood Grinches. House after house was a caricature in a winter's fable, silver mellophones, Good King Wenceslas, white globes blazing like votive candles, lambs nestling around a manger, wise men pointing to a star.

The merry luster of Peacock Lane contrasted the walk up Mount Tabor, icicle awnings and festive displays, stalactited Craftsmans and graupeled waterspouts, 45th coming all too soon, the cracked staircase sepulchered in manroot, the low garden wall, the jagged, misshapen Hawthorns.

The lights were on in the Mephistophelean House.

Ruefully I climbed the steps and opened the front door. Matthew sat on the couch. His boots melted on the floor. I closed the door, took off my coat, and hung it up to dry, and took out a box of soy milk that I stopped at lunch to buy.

"Houagh, houagh, houagh, houagh."

"How are you feeling?"

"Didn't go out."

"Not at all?"

Matthew kicked his boots under the couch.

"Nope."

"Why don't you go and see the Doctor?"

"I don't trust doctors."

"That's ridiculous."

I took a drink.

"What's that?"

"Soy milk. Never tried it before. I bought it at the food co-op."

I was certain Matthew would be impressed. Embarrassed by my habits I wanted to prove to Matthew that I could change.

"Wouldn't touch it with a 10 foot pole."

"What?"

"Soy creates phantom estrogens."

"Phantom estrogens?"

"Remember what cigarette companies called cancer in the nuclear age? Zephyrs. Mysterious, dust clouds on the human lung. Phantom estrogens are the zephyrs of today. Estrogen has penetrated our drinking supply, Ben. How else can you explain the explosion of reproductive cancer?"

"But it's organic."

"Ignorance is bliss, right Ben? Wrong. That's where I come in. I don't talk about 'conspiracy theories.' I talk about 'conspiracy fact.'"

"Conspiracy fact?"

Matthew's eyes burned.

"You see Ben, that's what I like about you. You listen to what I say. That's why I feel like I know you, even though we've just met. You're one of the few people, one of the *only* people I've ever met who isn't an idiot."

"But…"

"What I say is not opinion, Ben, but based on years of research. I know what I'm talking about. What I'm talking about is in the news, and I'll show you. The writing's on the wall, Ben. Nothing happens by coincidence."

Matthew's pupils were engorged.

The whites of his eyes were gone.

It was so cold you could see your breath.

"Ben, do you think we can turn the heat up?"

"But Matthew. You know these old Craftsmans. Single-paned windows. No insulation. Think of the cost. And just think," I maliciously appealed, "of the cost to the environment."

"You're right."

I poured the soy milk in the sink but there was nowhere to set the glass. A tower of Matthew's dishes overfilled the counter. I got a bottle of beer from the refrigerator and returned to the living room.

"Matthew, garbage is tomorrow. Do you want me to recycle your boxes?"

"Oh, yeah."

"How are we going to do utilities? Everything in my name?"

"Ok."

"So, I'll write five separate checks and you'll just pay me, then, each month?"

"You could pay the landlord too, so I could just write you one check."

"Oh. Ok."

"Oh, and if you wanted to work out a system where I cleaned the bathroom, like once a month or something, we could keep the place clean."

"It's going to take more than that to keep it clean, Matthew."

"It's clean as it is."

"That's because I cleaned it."

"I don't make messes."

"I don't think after what happened last night..."

"What happened?"

"I found some numbers on the wall in the basement. When I stopped to look at them, something strange happened."

"What?"

"It's hard to explain. The wall folded in on itself."

"Folded in on itself?"

"I…"

A knock rattled the floorboards.

Matthew jumped to his feet.

"What the hell was that?"

Matthew disappeared. The front door opened.

Matthew returned.

"There's no one on the porch."

"But..."

"Where did it come from?" but the question, almost half asked, was left unanswered.

We stared at each other.

"I'm not going down there."

"Ben," Matthew hesitated, "I didn't want to say anything, but, you left early this morning, right?"

"At six."

"I thought so. When I woke up, you were in my room."

"What?"

"You were standing over my bed. I looked at the clock. When I looked back, you were gone."

Matthew palmed a wad of tissue on the counter and

went upstairs to bed. I threw it away and turned off the light, locked the front door, and went upstairs. A purple haze drifted through the winding branches of the Walnut tree. There was a faint scarab of a moon.

I awoke in the middle of the night with a splitting headache. I went downstairs to get a cup of water and saw the curtain flapping at the top of the stairs. An angelic light shone through the second story window.

"How could Matthew have left the window open?"

I climbed the stairs. The curtain rustled, an ever intensifying radiance so brilliant I had to cover my eyes. When I reached out to close the window I heard the fluttering of wings.

The curtains fell.

The window was already closed.

4 · The Seven Year Curse

There's something in the House. I see It out of the corner of my eye. Matthew's changed. He's not the same. I can hear him arguing in his room. I hear other voices too, but nobody goes in, and nobody comes out.

Matthew screamed.

I ran downstairs.

He was on his hands and knees.

"Look at this!"

"What is that?"

I stuck my finger in a swath of slime.

"Protozoa, maybe?"

"Some kind of fast growing mold?"

"Wait a minute. It isn't over everything. Just our stuff. Everything else is dry."

"What?"

"Look!"

Our boxes, appliances, and dishes were covered in the same inexplicable excretion. The other surfaces, the cupboards, the floor, the wall, were dry.

"But the other stuff is dry. Why is it just our stuff?"

Matthew turned around.

There was something wrong.

"Did you know that the human body is composed of cells, and that every seven years, the atoms in your body are different? Atom by atom, you are not the same person you were seven years ago. In seven years the biological apparatus recycles itself anew. It's called the Seven Year Curse."

"The Seven Year Curse?"

"Every seven years you're a new person."

I didn't know what to make of the slime.

I returned to the grim little room.

"What's this?"

Matthew pulled a knife.

I jumped.

I hadn't heard Matthew come upstairs.

"I…I used it to cut a pizza."

"You mean, you used my knife?"

I had borrowed the Santoku for an instant, forgetting to replace it. I was sure it would go unnoticed in Matthew's tower of dishes.

"I'm sorry."

"Don't use my knife to cut meat."

"It was cheese pizza."

"Cheese is a meat product."

Matthew slammed the door.

I stared at the wainscoting.

The harder I tried, the worse Matthew made me feel.

I could hear him tramping in his room, pacing back and forth. There was a violent argument. Something fell on the floor.

"Matthew?"

I ran into the hall.

Matthew's door was closed.

"Matthew? Are you ok?"

I tried the door.

It was locked.

"Matthew?" I rested my ear against the door. "Are you ok?"

The door remained fast.

"Matthew!"

I stood in the hall with my hand on the wall and returned to the grim little room and got ready for work before checking my apps for the top listed posts on the news. I turned off the light and then opened the door to the scarious icicles melting, women in anoraks shoveling snow blocking the way I was heading.

"We're noticing you didn't get hit."

"Hit?"

"Some kind of prank."

I looked up the street. A slimy coating was plastered over the vehicles on 45th, the same inexplicable excretion I had seen in the Mephistophelean House.

"I think it was cornmeal and syrup."

"All the cars," the neighbor said, "except yours."

I looked over my shoulder.

The bio diesel was dry.

The MAX pulled into the Hollywood Station. I found a seat next to the window. I leaned back, chuckling at Matthew, festering in his room.

"Let your oats and soy save you, you twit. Oh wait, never mind, phantom estrogens."

I looked out the window.

"I don't care sitting in my chair if I am not polite. In delirium I ride the rails through cityscapes of white. What plague besets my roommate Matt, what pestilence, what blight? A bureaucrat of profane math, a tasker of redundant tasks, who's temperate teetotaling, conspiracy extolling, coy and cynic plight arouse a sickness hidden and forbidden fills my soul with spite?"

I chuckled at myself.

I chuckled at myself all day.

The MAX pulled into Hollywood at 4 o'clock. It was hailing. I raced up the hill and ducked under the bus shelter. Ice pellets ricocheted like culverins, an upturned graveyard of tables and chairs cobbling Belmont Square, the neon lights of an English pub and a rubble stone orange brick courtyard. I darted out into the down pouring hail and then made for the pub in the Square, the aroma of bangers, tobacco and vinegar saucing the chill winter air, dartboards, lithographs, nautical charts, a throwing arena with movable parts, spirits, lagers, rubicund ales, lists of IBU's bittering scales, a stout pyknic barkeep with cherry red cheeks was racking pint glasses with dishwasher streaks so I ordered a pilsner and sat on a stool, the pub decorated with tidings of yule, the beer on the bartop like subzero honey the barkeep accepted my folded wet money and hoisted the dish rack up on his broad back and set off down the hall under old Union Jack.

Someone was standing outside.

I squinted.

The hail was like diamonds.

"Matthew?"

I opened the door.

The cold air hit my face.

The courtyard was empty.

"Matthew?"

I penetrated the causeway. The professional offices were vacant. The parking lot was fronted by trees.

"I could have sworn it was him."

I cut across the parking lot.

A figure ran in the hail.

"Matthew?"

I cornered the old church and made my way through the easement up the cracked staircase, the Hawthorns a chantry in the snow.

The lights were on.

The front door was open.

"Matthew?"

I heard a noise.

"Matthew? Is that you?"

I climbed the stairs.

Matthew's door was closed.

"Matthew? Were you at Jacks?"

No reply.

"I'm coming in."

I turned the knob.

The door opened. The bed was made. The door to the

sleeping porch was open. I popped my head in.

Matthew was not in his room.

I walked over to the bureau.

The stick of yarrow was on the altar.

I picked it up.

It wasn't yarrow.

It was hair.

"What the..."

A bolt unlocked.

I went into the hall.

"Matthew?"

Muddy footprints led to the kitchen.

The white door was open.

"Matthew?"

Bespotted by floaters the white door congealed, salvos of hail, the music of spheres. I followed the footprints downstairs to the basement.

The circuit breaker was open.

#17 was off.

I reset #17.

Light shot under the door to the windowless chamber.

It was locked.

"Matthew, are you in there?"

Nothing.

"Matthew, is that you?"

Flies.

"Matthew, what are you doing in there?"

Silence.

Admonished, I banged on the door.

"Matthew, we're you at Jacks just now?"

Silence.

"What were you doing? Why didn't you come in?"

The door remained steadfast.

"Matthew!"

Matthew did not open the door.

I went upstairs. Muddy footprints were everywhere.

"Oh, damn. I forgot to take my shoes off. Now *I'm*

going to have to mop."

I fetched the mop and filled the bucket with water, following my muddy marks to the foyer. The staircase was wet.

"He must have mopped upstairs."

I climbed the freshly mopped stairs. I poked my head in the grim little room. A wet line ran through the abnormal closet room directly beneath the trap door.

"What the hell?"

I touched the trap door, the cold wet margin dripping, a piece breaking off from the decrepit stripping. I had a fell feeling regarding the ceiling, wondering what the mop marks were concealing.

"Why would Matthew mop the closet?"

I vellicated. I decided to go downstairs and confront my roommate, even if I had to break down the door. I returned to the basement and rapped on the door under the flue.

"Matthew, why did you mop my room?"

I could hear something moving.

"Matthew! Why did you mop my room? What's in the closet? What's behind the trap door?"

I stepped back.

The door to the windowless chamber opened.

It was empty.

"Matthew?"

Strings of digits upside-down, patterns of infinity, the black X like a snake unwound, the pink circle dark energy. I remembered Matthew's nightmare of the giant metal ball, the black X and bright pink circle side by side up on the wall. The circle glowed, a molten ball of liquid metal glass.

"This can't be happening."

The dumbwaiter was open.

A draft blew through the room.

I looked up the shaft.

There was a light in the attic.

"This can't be happening."

I took out my phone.

"911. How can I assist you?"

"My roommate's gone."

"Is he or she a missing person?"

"Yes."

"I'll connect you with the police. Just a moment."

The line clicked.

"Portland Police."

"Yes. My roommate is gone. He's missing."

"How long has he been gone?"

When was the last time I had seen Matthew?

I couldn't remember.

"Three days."

"Three days?"

"Yes."

"And your name?"

I gave the dispatcher my personal information.

"What's the address?"

"1331, S.E. 45th."

"Could you repeat that?"

"1331, S.E. 45th."

"There's no such address."

"What?"

"There's no such address."

Static.

"Hello?"

"Is anyone there?"

I looked at the screen.

I had no bars.

"Hello? Is there anyone there?"

"What's the physical location of the residence?"

I put the receiver to my ear.

"It's…it's a couple houses south of 45th and Main."

"The detectives will be there shortly."

"Thank you."

I pressed end.

The call had already ended.

The hail let up. I stood on the porch looking up at the Mephistophelean House. There were windows in the gable that I didn't recognize. The Mephistophelean House appeared to have increased in size. Beneath the wide-capped ridge vent where the soffit underlie I could hear the noxious chirring of the buzzing of the flies.

An unmarked cruiser pulled onto 45th. Two plain clothes detectives got out and cut through the easement, climbing the steps to the porch.

"Are you the one that called about the missing person?"

"Yes."

"This is Detective Morris. I'm Detective Gamble."

"I called about my roommate, Matthew Pierce. He got sick and disappeared."

"What sort of illness?"

My forehead dripped.

I wiped my brow.

"I'm not sure."

I kept seeing things out of the corner of my eye, deformities, anomalies, spots on the wall, things that hadn't been there before.

The detectives didn't seem to notice.

"Are those your boots?"

Matthew's boots were on the floor, dripping with melting snow.

"Yes."

"What are those?"

I looked at my boots.

"I changed."

"Take us to his room."

"What time did he disappear?"

"It would have been Saturday night."

"Did you call his family?"

"I don't know if he had any family. I mean, he never spoke of any. He never had anyone over."

"We'll take what information you have."

"I have three numbers. One is the place he was living before."

"Before?"

"We just moved in."

"Oh?"

"The second is the number of the landlord. The third is his."

Detective Morris accepted the numbers.

"Let's see his room."

"It's this way."

I led the detectives upstairs.

The room was as I left it.

"In there," I pointed.

The detectives put on gloves. Detective Gamble pointed to the sleeping porch.

"What's that?"

"It's some kind of extra room."

The detective opened the door and went inside.

"What is it Terry," Detective Morris pulled a canister from a leather bag and sprayed the floor, chair, and wall.

Detective Gamble popped his head through the doorway.

"Did you notice anything strange or out of the ordinary? Other than this sickness?"

I shrugged my shoulders.

"Not to my knowledge."

"Anything?"

"Negative."

"Fingerprints?" I asked.

"Body residuals."

"Ahh."

"Where was the last place you saw him?"

"Probably the basement."

I blenched.

Why had I said that?

"All right. Give me the details. What were you talking about?"

"He was building something, some kind of personal waste recycling system."

"Was building? You talk about him as if he were dead."

"Gone."

"Do you have any reason to believe he's deceased?"

"I don't know what to believe."

"Let's see the basement."

I unbolted the white door. The fan was on. The door to the windowless chamber was open.

"It's damp down here."

"Where did see him last?"

I pointed.

"Inside there?"

"Turn on the lights."

"The lights are on."

"Oh."

"What is that?"

"It's a dumbwaiter."

Detective Gamble stared at the black X and pink circle. The other detective set his case on the ground and withdrew the canister, spraying the floor.

"It's no use."

I led the detectives upstairs.

Detective Gamble handed me a card.

"You can reach Detective Morris through this number."

"Thank you."

"Anything else you can tell us about him?"

"I hardly knew the guy."

I stood in the Hawthorns, looking up at the Mephistophelean House. Although the detectives found no trace of Matthew there was one place they hadn't searched.

"Ogemtel."

I snatched the phone from my pocket and dialed the landlord's number.

The line rang twice.

A recorded message played.

The line was disconnected.

5 · The Investigation

I know I am not mad, but now I am alone and It knows I am alone. The longer I stay, the less It bothers to hide. Even in the light of day I am perturbed by vague irrationalities, things I can't directly perceive, memories of things which never took place. I pretend not to notice It, but It knows I am pretending.

I don't remember how I got to bed.

I woke up in the grim little room. Beads of water trickled from the awning, rain intermixed with snow. The ice was in full retreat.

The pigeons were gone.

Matthew's door was ajar.

I went to the bathroom and splashed some water on my face.

My eyes were burning.

"My eyes…"

I looked in the mirror.

There was someone there.

A robe hung on a hook.

"Jeez."

I went downstairs. The kitchen seemed different. Streaks mottled the linoleum floor, imperfections in the corbels and rope molding, pilasters and trim out of place, as if the entire House had been taken apart and put back together again.

I got a bag of coffee from the fridge. The coffeemaker

percolated. I poured a cup. The milk mixed with the coffee.

"What the…"

A face appeared.

I blinked.

It was gone.

The kitchen elongated, the metal bowl on the counter, the scuffed refrigerator, the chipped enamel cooker, the gleaming white door, my elongated face in the reflection, something behind me, as tall as Death, reaching out.

"I've got to get out of here."

There was a new sapling in the yard, one that had not been there the night before. I shuddered at the coincidence of Matthew's disappearance, noticing a section of newly turned earth, large enough where another might lie.

Bus #14 roared up Hawthorne. Trustifarians in freeform locks unloaded Vanagons of second hand brands. GenX go-getters in heathered fleece sweaters avoided the hollas of signature gatherers. A stout bearded lady and brown basset hound brayed for ten dollar bills with a hat on the ground. A halcyon mural and bright coffee shop stood next to the Psychics and Trimet bus stop. A circle of writers sat down to a meeting so I queued in line while they interchanged greetings. I ordered a Depthcharge with white pumpkin crème and sat down by the steaming espresso machine.

A game of chess was played. A player broke his castle and the rook went unopposed. The other took the bait and left his knight and pawns exposed. I sat next to the root ball table Depthcharge in my hand, thinking of the Weeping Tree inside the forest of sand. The Depthcharge had been flavored with a cappuccino glaze, caffeinated chocolate candy corroding the haze.

"What happened to Matthew doesn't have to happen to me."

I took out my phone and tapped the mic icon.

"Property history Multnomah County."

I queried the address 1331 SE 45th, Portland Oregon in

the search bar. The tax records registered two results, a property deed and pdf.

The deed was a type written document, notarized at the turn of the twentieth century, bearing an earlier date. It was signed by a Doctor Maximilian Kilgore.

"Doctor Kilgore?"

The pawn advanced, forking the bishop and rook.

The second link was a lien on the property at 1331 SE. 45th, dated 1917.

"Maximilian Kilgore, the grantee listed in the first section of the lien, having been secured by a private trust, stated as valuable consideration the property of 1331, SE 45th, to Roland Andrews."

I stared at the touchscreen.

"The lien is a hundred years old."

Maximilian Kilgore and Roland Andrews returned two million results. I sifted like an inept cleric in a decrepit repository, drinking my Depthcharge, stumbling across an abstract from an academic database of electronic articles with a reference to Doctor Maximilian Kilgore.

"Of a considerably more questionable nature remain the endeavors of Doctor Maximilian Kilgore, 1856-1917, cofounder of the Oregon State Board of Eugenics. Little is recorded, despite having been the Superintendent of the House on Asylum Road for nine years, from 1908-1917, and a Representative of the Oregon State Legislature, from 1912-1917. Records point to Doctor Kilgore as the primary medical advisor guiding the creation of the Board of Eugenics in 1917. The Board, confirming a common practice of the era, empowered superintendents of mental institutions to sterilize inmates so that their inferior traits would not be passed onto resulting generations. Doctor Kilgore, it appears, sterilized with impunity such that he was reviled even by his own contemporaries. Of the 174 patients entrusted in his care only one escaped, and he, on appeal to the Oregon State Supreme Court. Doctor Kilgore disappeared in 1917. The House on Asylum Road was closed in 1920. All state mental institutions were consolidated into one central facility, the Oregon State Insane Asylum, in 1921."

The property lien on the Mephisthopelean House was dated 1917, the year the Doctor disappeared.

"The House on Asylum Road?"

The shop receded, people talking without speaking, echoes distant and unreal, potted plants with moving roots were cracking through the brushstone tile, spoons and forks, stalks and leaves, the wind blowing through the trees, a figure digging on their knees under the chilblained Hawthorns trees.

"A private trust…"

The delicious aroma of cinnamon pastry, coffee, and perfume, the clinking of glasses, music, voices, steam spouting from the espresso machine.

The pawn took the bishop.

I took a shot from the Depthcharge.

"Board Eugenics Maximilian Kilgore."

The search produced a result from the Portland Public Library, an entry entitled The Narcissus Effect. Under the subject line it listed eugenics and The House on Asylum Road. The author was Doctor Maximilian Kilgore.

"The Narcissus Effect."

I clicked the call number.

The book was in.

I looked at the clock.

The king was cornered in his castle.

Matthew's keys were on the bureau. Wasting no time I fired the bio diesel and took Hawthorne downtown, the Willamette River leaking like brown paint under the steel truss of the Hawthorne Bridge. Neon signs lit up Main Street. I rolled uptown and found a spot on 10th, printed a ticket, and stickered the window.

A surreal hush permeated the Downtown Public Library. The wrought iron clock read 6:59. I climbed the Tennessee marble staircase to the second floor and looked up 'The Narcissus Effect' on a terminal. There was just enough time to deposit the call number at the desk before the library closed.

A warning flashed on the screen.

"Just a moment," the librarian disappeared into the rook.

Columns with scrolls and acanthus leaves vaulted a field of arches. I looked at the portraits on the wall. A bell rang. Two security guards climbed the stairs. I looked at the clock.

It still read 6:59.

The librarian returned.

"Although this title is checked in, I can't seem to lay my hands on it."

"Lost?"

"Not lost. It's here, somewhere, but just where, I couldn't say."

"Oh."

"Let's cross index the subjects and see what we can come up with."

One by one the lights shut off. The portraits in the colonnade frothed blue and white, jagged mountain peaks, raging waterfalls, tiny figures braving the vast unforgiving panorama.

"What are you guys looking for?"

"Guys?"

The guards were heading downstairs.

"My mistake. What specifically were you looking for?"

"Eugenics, Doctor Maximilian Kilgore."

"Just a moment. I'm noticing a common thread throughout the subject indices. The House on Asylum Road."

"Yes. The House on Asylum Road. That's it."

"Just a moment. Carlin College has that title in a collection. I'd go there if I were you."

"All right."

"But you can't."

"Oh?"

"It's a private college."

"I see."

"Hey, are you alright?"

"Why?"

"There's something wrong with your eyes."

I heard somebody on the stairs and stopped to let them pass, but there was nobody there, the lights were off and it was black, yet every time I turned I heard footsteps behind my back, a presence treading in my wake no longer holding back, and though I tried ignoring the clock hanging on the wall, it seemed to me it looked a lot like Matthew's metal ball, the time that wrought the iron hands that broke the center line, a time I knew I need not see in order to divine.

6:59.

6 · The Gargoyles

A gust rocked the cantilever truss of the Ross Island Bridge. The aerial tram swung over the Terwilliger Curves like a drogue in a wall cloud. The cable-stayed pylons of South Waterfront were a menagerie of steel and glass. I pumped the accelerator, looking into the rear view mirror.

My eyes were bloodshot.

The argent yards on Milwaukie Ave were rendered in melting snow. A cab carted hopper wagons and road railers under the Bybee overpass. The bio diesel circled Crystal Springs Lake and parked in the rhododendron garden across from Carlin College.

The dorms overlooked the parking lot. I followed the path through the trees. Across an embankment was a light. A lamp post illuminated a bridge.

I heard the sound of wings.

I looked up.

Had I been mistaken?

Snow dusted the ferns.

I strained my ears. The lamp post hummed. My eyes grew accustomed to the dark. The flush cuts and root collars of shore pines and vine maple secreted ghastly silhouettes.

A branch overturned.

I could see something moving in the trees.

A pule cut the ruddy pail.

I hurried across the bridge. The path opened onto an old dorm block. The dorm block had a Sallyport with iron lanterns. A snouted figure perched atop the cornice with wings like a bat.

"What is that?"

I stood under the Sallyport looking up, razor sharp talons, slits and horns, a trickle of snow melting from its misshapen maw.

"Gargoyles."

A second gargoyle with pincer-like talons girted a scaly tail. Out of place on the weathered façade the gargoyles were cratered in glass. The quad was empty so I crossed the Sallyport, eager to be on my way. I was about to turn the corner when I heard the same sycophantic pule I had heard in the wood.

The light was playing tricks on my eyes. The gargoyles seemed to be moving, a third facing my way (hadn't they been facing the other way?) staring down, directly overhead, a fourth and a fifth, runoff blotting the cornice, a sixth and seventh (where had they all come from?), lantern-lit scales and thorny brows bristling, snouts contracting, jaws machinating.

"Oh God."

One by one the gargoyles turned, pillared in flecks of snow.

The Administration Building was locked. Across from Llyr Circle I spotted the Library.

The library door would not budge.

"Damn."

An undergrad crossed the commons and slipped a phone over the reader. The library door opened. I followed, the door locking behind me.

No one looked up.

The atrium was sedate. I approached the circulation desk and asked where I might find help locating my title. The student at the desk pointed me to the reference section.

"Excuse me, I'm looking for information on the House on Asylum Road. Two doctors in particular. Here are their names." I wrote 'The Narcissus Effect' and the doctors on an index card and gave it to the librarian.

The library was crowded. Every seat was taken, undergrads hunched over secret treatises, typing on tablets, scrawling line after line just to cross it out and start all over again.

"Special Collections," the librarian said. "You'll need a consultant." The librarian wrote a series of numbers on the back of the card. "It will be about 5 minutes. You have time to find your other titles. Go to the first lower level."

"Thanks."

I checked the map before heading downstairs. The first number, a dissertation, and the second, a journal, were in adjacent aisles. I sat down at an empty table. The dissertation was entitled the "Oregon Board of Eugenics." I turned to the introduction and read.

"From 1917-1963, the Oregon Board of Eugenics regularly sterilized epileptics, criminals and degenerates who were deemed to be a menace to society. Native Americans were also sterilized. The Oregon Board, like others across the nation, believed they were protecting the human gene pool by weeding out sub-humans. Bolstered by the 1927 Supreme Court case Buck vs. Bell which legitimized forced sterilization of the institutionalized, nearly 3000 Oregonians were operated upon, many dying from complications, well into 1967. The last forcible sterilization occurred in Oregon in 1981. It is not known how many Native Americans were sterilized in Oregon, but it is estimated to be in the tens of thousands."

I flipped to the index. There was an entry for Kilgore. I turned to the seventh chapter and located the reference.

"Although common practice in private institutions across the eastern seaboard, the practice of eugenic sterilization in Oregon was pioneered by two doctors, Maximilian Kilgore and Roland Andrews at The House on Asylum Road, a private sanitarium in East Portland. The House on Asylum Road was shut down in 1920. In private institutions like the House on Asylum Road questionable medical practices such as deep sleep theory, insulin shock, and electroconvulsive therapy predicated the rise of state sponsored disease manufacturing in 20th century schools for the handicapped and the clandestine inoculations on U.S. armed forces continuing to this day."

"Deep Sleep Theory?"

I set the dissertation aside and opened the journal, flipping to 'Eugenics Records Mysteriously Disappear.'

"The records of institutionalized patients housed in private and public asylums were destroyed in 2002. All paper documents were shredded. No electronic copies were made. The entire history of 2650 interred Oregonians in mental institutions during the era of the Oregon Board of Eugenics were expunged, along with all State documentation, including the whereabouts of the remains."

"What have I gotten myself into?"

The silence was broken by two undergrads in the next aisle.

"Everything in the universe, the planets, stars, and galaxies account for less than 5% of what is really out there. 95% of the universe is a mystery. We say it's a quarter dark matter, three quarters dark energy, but what does that even mean? What does it mean when we can only describe what is, by what it is not?"

"Are there other universes?"

"Quantum mechanics predicts the many-worlds interpretation. There are an infinite number of increasing, divergent realities for everything that has, is, and will happen. Roll a die and create six alternate realities, the one that came up, and the five that didn't. Imagine how quickly the possibilities stack up."

"But if that is true, and there are alternate universes, then there must be an infinite number of alternate universes."

"Possibly."

"Do they all share the same laws of physics?"

"In a way. The structure and the constants are the same."

"What I really mean is, is it possible to travel from one universe to another? For example, could I travel to an alternate reality?"

"All universes are connected through quantum interference."

"What's quantum interference?"

"Quantum interference is a force, like entropy, emitted by each universe upon the next. It is like throwing a stone in a pond. The pond is the multiverse, where all universes, all realities, come together. Cast a stone. The ripples are quantum interference, the borders of different universes, one inside the other."

"All universes are connected through quantum interference?"

"Yes."

"Our idea of time, and history, is corrupt, then, isn't it?"

"What do you mean?"

"Like a stone in a pond. That which happened meets that which didn't?"

"Well…"

"Instead of physics think of history. Now, as we know it, isn't really a result of the past, is it? Now is the quotient of quantum interference."

"I'm not sure what you mean…"

"What if that which never happened exerted a heavier force, a greater quantum interference, upon now, than what occurred? What if now was the product of all the things which never happened? Your 95%. The force of quantum interference is the result of all the sides **not** rolled on the die, the things which never occurred, the eventualities which never took place. Look at the ripples in the pond. See the circles expand, over and over, like history repeating itself? Our idea of now, the present moment, our place in history, is just a ripple on the pond, a disturbance where alternate realities coincide the moment they diverge."

"Well, I…"

"If all the things which never happened directly influence that which is happening now, how could there ever be such a thing as free will?"

"You cast the stone."

"What happened to your eyes?"

Something clawed my shoulder.

I jumped.

A nefarious librarian harkened down the aisle.

"The viewing area is this way."

The librarian proceeded down an unlit hallway and swiped a key card. A heavy metal door opened. A reading room was framed in manuscripts, historical leaflets, woodcuts, and daguerreotypes. The librarian unlocked a drawer and set a small, hardbound edition on a table.

"This," the librarian lowered, "is not a book that sees the light of day. They consolidated before the purge. This is all that remains of a private trust."

"A private trust?"

My throat tightened.

"But you know all about that…"

The nether worldly volume sat on the table, deckle edges tinged in gold. On the cover, emblazoned in ink, was the Weeping Tree.

The metal door slammed shut. The volume clattered like a block of lead flipping open to the title page.

The Narcissus Effect
A Study in Human Nature
1908
Doctor Maximilian Kilgore

Will Science bring us closer to God, or God closer to us? God created us in His own image. How may we recognize him, reflected in ourselves? As good and evil rage their war inside the human soul, alliances of Sin and Science rush to fill the hole. Medicating symptoms proffers broken guarantees; that which plagues us as a race is far worse than disease.

Excise the individual. Another is infected. Contagion spreads. We are left with plague. There is no shortage of individuals. A billion souls now roam this world at war. Imagine a world twice as crowded. What potential for violence would eviscerate the spirit of the times? A world twice as crowded, again? Perpetual war? A war that never ends? Just as there is no shortage of men, there is no shortage of Sin. Consider the metaphor of the diseased mind. Were the world the mind of a psychopath, would not each individual person represent a passing mania? Each face, the face of madness? Such an unchecked, consensual reality is the scourge of Man and the fate of the individual.

Unless we operate.

But how to operate upon the soul of man?

This study identifies a series of procedures to be implemented in Institutions of Public Health across the nation in order to address fundamental moral phenomena in a systematic undertaking. Operate upon a man, does he not bleed? Operate upon the soul of man to solve the riddle of his bleeding. Evil conspires to subsume the human soul. Science prevails a new City of God. Tangled are the webs we weave inside the human mind. What horror might befall us all, deep and dark inside? Where is soul, where is disease, that which makes us ill at ease, when one peers in a mirror has there ever been one dearer, an invention of one's mind, a distant find drawn ever nearer?

In my mind Doctor Maximilian Kilgore addressed the Infernal Legislature, beaming like a beacon in mankind's darkest hour, the world at war, the Infernal Legislators cloying, the gavel falling, the assembly rising out of their seats, boisterous calls from both sides of the aisle for the esteemed Doctor to chair the Oregon Board of Eugenics, protestations of delight and affirmation, compacts of solidarity, the Doctor echoing across the capitol dome, "but my friends, my colleagues, my brothers in arms, fear not, haste hath dutifully been employed. Work has already begun."

The netherworldly volume rested on the table. The brown dust jacket was unscuffed, dentelle trig and true, the offset print and bastard title bounded in fresh glue; although the book was very old the text block case was new, the untrimmed leaves in mint condition, endpaper see-through.

"I've got to get out of here."

Flurries of snow pocketed the quad outside the Library. Something was missing from the old dorm block. The Sallyport was pockmarked, dappled abrasions cutting the length of the cornice.

The gargoyles were gone.

Had I imagined the whole thing?

I heard the rustling of wings.

I looked up.

The lanterns on the Sallyport cast transmogrifications over the dappled maculation. The light played tricks on my eyes.

I followed the path through the wood and was about to cross the bridge when I noticed a gargoyle on the post.

"I don't remember…"

The wood was silent.

The gargoyle rose on its haunches.

The lamppost hummed.

The creek gurgled.

The trees swayed.

There was no wind.

"Must have imagined it."

The gargoyle unloosed a guttural caterwaul.

A stone hammer face-planted my skull on the rail. I reached out but my hands didn't work. I fell on my knees, bleating wings rising in a field of stars, blood pouring from my mouth, static in my ears.

"Argh."

I stumbled across the bridge.

The old dorm block poked through the trees.

"Oh no."

My head spun.

A lump formed.

A shadow sailed over the treetops.

There were more of them now.

"There's got to be another way around."

I snaked through the ferns. The creek faded.

"Must be pretty high up."

The wood was silent.

I looked up.

There were gargoyles in the tree.

One went for my face.

"Argh!"

I strafed over the embankment twenty five feet to the creek bed below.

My life flashed before my eyes.

If I had a second chance, I would have said I never saw the Mephistophelean House. If I knew then what I know now, I'd have never gone inside. If I had my life back, I would ignore the trap door, the abnormal closet, the windowless chamber.

But as I fell a root jutted from the escarpment and I grabbed hold, slamming against the lip. I kicked my legs and turned myself around, pitching like a fish on a hook

The gargoyles echeloned. Dagger horns and crooked pincers gashed my hands and arms, maws of tuff and glassy spikes with muzzles made of thorns, a gargoyle lit upon the root and set to rip it out, I caught the devil with my knee and smashed its bony snout.

The root slipped.

"No!"

The gargoyle fell onto the rocks.

I scrambled up the lip. A pair of gargoyles volplaned, mantling the murder with their spiny wings. I kicked one over the ledge but the other latched on, clawing its way up my leg. I got up and ran, dashing it against the rocks, but instead of smashing to pieces it recoiled, yawping in the duff.

The primal instinct for survival kicked in. I made for the road. The ground was wet and it was hard to see. In the distance I saw a street lamp. I followed the tree line back to the parking lot and jumped inside the bio diesel.

The parking lot was empty.

There were no scratches on my leg.

My shirt was dry.

"This can't be happening."

I wrested the phone from my pocket.

A raspy voice answered.

"Yeah?"

"Jonsrud?"

"Listen. I'm coming up. I've got Matthew's car."

"Don't tell me you're bringing *that* prick..."

"Matthew's gone."

"What?"

"It's the House. There's something in the House."

7 · The Thing at the Ranch

Colossal rolling thrones stoked diesel plumes, log carriers, ballast tractors, heavy haulers, parking lots, zoned developments, empty fields, trees, brush and grass. I cranked the heat, the oncoming traffic a pure white snake. The Capitol was unobservable from the freeway, a metered blur breaching the freeway wall.

A state police cruiser merged onto the interstate.

I tapped the brakes.

"Great. Just great."

The lights flashed.

I huffed, gripping the wheel. The cruiser shot forward, chicaning around the bend. I stepped on the accelerator, unnerved.

What had I to fear?

What crime had I committed?

I exited onto Kuebler Road and headed east, the bio diesel's high-beams illuminating a winding, country road. A manufactured home was for sale. The name on a mailbox was scratched out. A fence led nowhere.

I looked at the digital clock on the leather dashboard. I had been driving for 70 minutes.

Sublimity
Population
2709

It was hard to keep the car on the road. The road pitched without warning. I stared down the high beams, accelerating. The familiar, clipped milepost indicated the private road to the Jonsrud ranch, a tree farm separated from a pasture by an electric fence for a quarter of a mile.

The estate was bathed in floodlights. I circled the turnaround and parked next to the shop. A pint-sized Feist yipped frantically on a chain, strangling itself by the neck. A Deerhound named Calapooya emerged from the barn, growling. I took a knee and extended my hand, beckoning the good-natured, loyal hound, Jonsrud's hunting companion, and my personal favorite.

The Deerhound bared its fangs.

"Calapooya?"

The Deerhound snarled.

"Calapooya? Don't you know me?"

The Feist barked irascibly.

"What's gotten into you guys?"

Calapooya lunged. I backed into the barn. I could hear a struggle, the chain snap, the dogs taking off.

Hampshire, Suffolk, and Southdowns huddled around a manger. A pyramid of hay bales stretched up to the rafters where a tom cat licked fir. I ducked my head over the fence post and looked outside.

The dogs were gone.

"Hmm. Must have slipped the chain."

The chain was cut in two.

An electrified fence shadowed the ridge. The lights in the arena were on. I followed the dirt road looking up at the night sky.

Inside the arena Jonsrud was roped to a 1300 pound palomino.

"Canter."

The horse cantered.

"Good boy."

Jonsrud snapped the whip.

"Halt."

The horse pulled up.

"Good boy."

"Good boy Jonsrud," I said.

"You're here," Jonsrud stroked the horse, 16 hands bristling with muscle. The palomino inspected my pockets with its mutinous lips.

"Hey," I exclaimed, "Why don't you whip him and say 'Bad Boy?'"

"He's curious."

"He's a pervert."

The palomino knelled.

"He's fat. He needs to lose some weight."

"Good boy," I pet the horse.

"You know Ben, one of these days we're going to have to halter you up and teach you to canter."

I laughed.

"I thought," Jonsrud lowered his voice, "you said you weren't going to bring that prick."

"Matthew's gone."

"But…"

The gate banged against the post.

The palomino reared, pile driving Jonsrud into the dirt. I grasped the reigns but the palomino's hooves sliced the marker.

"Jonsrud!"

The vainglorious berserker rose on its haunches. There was nothing I could do. I let go of the reigns. It was too late. The rope locked around my wrist. I was pulled under.

The hooves descended. Jonsrud grabbed the halter and wrenched it sideways, cradling its jowls and poll. The quarter horse slipped the halter and cast him aside, bolting around the arena.

"There's something out there."

I picked myself up.

"Whoah, boy."

The horse doubled back.

"He's spooked."

"We'll never get him now."

Jonsrud withdrew a pack of cigarettes and headed for the gate.

"Let's take a look."

The palomino kicked up plumes of silt, Jonsrud's cigarette smudging a blurred line. We stood outside, silos dotting the forest like a silver city. Far below we could hear the Feist yipping across the field.

"There's nothing here."

"I could have sworn I saw someone."

"Matthew's gone. The detectives came."

"Detectives?"

I told Jonsrud about the pattern on the basement floor, the trap door, the upside-down numbers, the gargoyles, Doctor Maximilian Kilgore. To return in my mind to the Mephistophelean House was to return to the windowless chamber, the place in the wall where the black X and pink circle came together.

"He's calmed down," Jonsrud said. The palomino drank from a trough. "I'll put him in the paddock."

Jonsrud wedged his cigarette in the dirt and led the palomino into the paddock, snatching a fresh bale of alfalfa. He replaced the hose and closed the door, joining me outside.

"What about the dogs?"

"Coyote's no match for a Deerhound. They'll come back after they chased off whatever it was."

We followed the road back to the veranda. A marble bar, metal chairs and glass tables were arranged around a Cartesian fountain. Jonsrud opened the French doors and we entered a granite-topped kitchen. Portraits of Jonsrud as a younger man hung on the wall of the great room, a staircase abutting a stone mantle, the skull of an ox in its center.

Jonsrud built a fire. He put the poker in the rack and proceeded to the bar.

"Freshen your drink, governor?"

"Certainly."

Chestnut flasks and Benedictine bottles bedecked a demilune bar. Jonsrud poured two highballs, handing me one.

"There could be explanations for the things you describe," he suggested, sinking onto a brown leather chaise. "Normal situations misinterpreted."

"Such as?"

"You said yourself the basement smelled like gas. There's your black X and pink circle."

"I've thought about that. What about the other things?"

"The water in the basement. Foundations warp. The building's over a hundred years old. The other things, like the billowing curtains, could have been dreams. You woke up in the middle of the night, right? Who's to say you didn't dream the whole thing? Matthew could be back by now, for all you know. How much do you know about him, anyway?"

"I hardly knew the guy."

"What about the gargoyles?"

"It doesn't make sense. If there is something in the House, how could it follow you?"

The poker hung on the rack.

"I don't know," Jonsrud ruminated, "people disappear every day. There are over a hundred thousand missing persons registered by the FBI. One hundred thousand. Are the supernatural to blame? Is our nation being shanghaied by specters? Kidnaped by corpses?"

Jonsrud craned his neck.

"Jonsrud?"

The color drained from his face.

He stared up, profoundly still.

"Jonsrud?"

The fire blazed.

Jonsrud went over to the poker.

"What was that, you were you saying?"

"Are we to presume, Doctor..."

"Doctor?"

"Just a figure of speech, but are we to presume, on this

melancholy moon, that the dead are taking our place? That soon every house, a Mephistophelean House, bereft of the human race? And that facets of you, and the things that you do, deep inside are becoming erased, just a matter of time with a corrupted mind, disappearing without a trace."

"Jesus Christ, you sound like Matthew."

In the light of the hearth I raised my glass.

The fire burned richly.

I looked through the window.

The forest was dark.

The stars were cold.

"Some things require a leap of faith."

The poker glinted.

One by one, the stars blotted out.

A dog barked.

There was the sound of a struggle.

A bone crunching scream.

"Calapooya!"

"Don't open the door."

"Calapoya's back."

"I told you it's not Calapooya. I brought It here, with me."

"It's Calapoyya. I'll open the door."

"Jesus Christ, don't open **that** door."

The fire cracked.

The door opened.

I made for the poker.

8 · Moving Out

I sat up.
It was day.
Jonsrud was gone.
The poker was missing.
"Jonsrud?"
My head ached.
"What happened?"
The mansion was empty.
I checked the second floor.
The den was unoccupied.
The bedrooms were vacated.
I stood in the office looking out over the ranch.
"Jonsrud!"
I called Jonsrud.
He didn't answer.
"Maybe he went somewhere."
The pickup was next to the shop.
"Truck's here."
I checked the barn.
The dogs were gone.
I walked over to the arena.
The palomino drank from the trough.
"Where in the hell did everybody go?"
The air was stagnant.
The trees were still.
I could not remember.

I went back to the house.

I sat in the great room.

Jonsrud did not appear.

"I can't remember!"

I looked at the floor.

The sofa did not cast a shadow.

Nor did the table.

The hutch, recliner, and shelves were shadowless.

Not even I cast a shadow.

The ashes in the hearth rustled.

"The poker. Calapooya…"

Light poured through the window.

"I brought It here, with me…"

The evergreens swayed on the hill, just as they always had. Just as they always would. In the evergreens I stood next to a pond, holding a stone.

"Let me go."

In a white room with a white carpet, it is easy to see when something is out of place. Especially when there is a shadow on a day when no shadows are cast.

"Wherever I go."

"Whatever I do."

"I'll never be free."

"***You'll be there too.***"

The surface of the pond was still.

I could see my reflection.

It was there.

Behind me.

It was reaching out.

I grasped the stone.

"There are a lot of things in the basement that need to go."

"Knickknacks, keepsakes, even a couple of cans of gas."

I had nothing to lose.

"It's so nice to come to Home to a fire…even when there isn't a fireplace."

A hellish scream riled the horses in the field.

The bio diesel accelerated down the dirt road past the clipped signpost, tailpipe burning a bio-chemical trail through Sublimity. A colorless sun hung over the Willamette Valley. I-5 topknotted the Marquam Bridge and merged onto the Banfield. I drove in a stupor, planning my next move.

"It knows I'm coming. I have to be quick. No milling about. I'll get what I need, pack the car, set the house on fire…"

I looked in the rear view mirror.

"If I lost control, and something else was pulling the strings, would I know? If IT was me, and I was a stranger to myself, at what point did It take over? When did I stop calling the shots? Why go back? Isn't that what It wants? Isn't that what It's wanted, all along?"

Logic painted a precarious causeway over a chasm of despair. The overcast sky stretched infinitely overhead. I stepped on the gas, rub strip skirting the freeway wall, accelerator curling like an adder, the engine cutting in and out, wheels losing momentum, emergency lights on, the gauge at 300 degrees.

"You've got to be kidding me."

I pulled into Laurelhurst. Smoke wisped into the cabin. I got out and popped the hood. The engine block was cracked. The bio diesel would have to be towed.

Drizzle eroded the last remnants of white on Cesar Chavez Avenue, the golden Maid of Orleans buffeted in rain. An adumbrate penumbra buried Belmont Square and the old church, a bitter chill descended still enshrouded in a mist, Hawthorn thorns, and black acorns, the windows empty and forlorn, I climbed the stairs into despair's capricious moldy gut, and opened the unholy door and stepped with fear inside, waiting for the Mephistophelean House to seethe my soul awry, but nothing came from in the House and at the door I stood, wishing I had moved into another neighborhood.

The Deerhound was waiting.

"Calapooya?"

It perked Its head.

The white door unbolted.

"Jonsrud? Is that you?"

The Deerhound tramped into the kitchen.

The white door was open.

I called at the top of the stairs.

"Jonsrud? Is this some kind of joke?"

Paws crossed the floor. Water trickled down the wall. The pump whirred. I poked my head under the flue inside the windowless chamber.

The Deerhound was gone.

Water spilled from the trough. The floor was dry. The black X and pink circle shone like a bloody sun. I studied the upside-down numbers on the wall, 174 lines repeated over and over.

"174, 174, where have I heard that number before? Shouldn't have come down here. Shouldn't have come back at all. X marks the spot. The Doctor's private trust..." I reconsidered. "Quantum interference, like a stone in a pond. The ripples are the borders between that which happened and all the things which could of happened, but didn't."

I stared at the black X and pink circle. The black X marked the spot on the wall where the two sides came together. If I stood a little closer to the wall, the black X superimposed the pink circle. If I stood in front of it, the black X and pink circle came together.

I stood in the windowless chamber, though it would have been difficult to call myself me. Pieces of a mirror lie on the floor.

"The mirror. The red box. Wait. The red box. It's gone. The red box isn't here."

It was like a dream. Upstairs was bright and new. I went into the hall. The front door was open. Main Street was abandoned.

The Deerhound yowled under the Walnut tree. A pigeon fluttered in the grass. The other pigeons looked down at it pitilessly.

It had a broken snout.

The horse rings on Main were hitched to their roundings. Slush melted in leaf-packed puddles. Chimneys pitched columns of ash. I followed the Deerhound up the hill. There were no people. Some houses I recognized. Some were dark. Some were empty.

The Deerhound ducked into an alley. Goatsbeard and Grape Holly choked the cinder cone spillway. The Deerhound pulled farther and farther ahead. I fell farther and farther behind. The alley opened onto 55th. A barbican permitted access to a promontory with hemicycles and apses, the outline of a byzantine presidio visible through the hedge. The Deerhound passed through a metal turnstile with a cornerstone which bore the nameplate, 'The House on Asylum Road.'

"The House on the Hill."

I fell on the bank.

"I am dead."

The clay eroded. Rain spilled into a sinkhole. I lay by the sinkhole on the edge of an endless reservoir of tears.

"Quantum interference. All the things which never happened. That's why It follows me wherever I go. The black X and pink circle are a nadir."

Could I return through the nadir?

Back through the black X and pink circle?

I stared up at the House on Asylum Road.

Rain beat on the corrugated roof of Northgate. A guardhouse commanded the interstice. Inside the guard house an ugly man sat on a stool, staring through the grill.

"Hello," I rapped. "I'm here to see the Doctor."

I noticed the chronic lesions of sarcoidosis, a hyperkeratinised scar running from crown to ear. Tiny puncture wounds dotted the superior and inferior temporal lines of his left parietal bone.

"I said I'm here to the see the Doctor."

"Doctor!" the ugly man drooled.

"Yes."

I waited.

"Doctor?"

"That's what I said. The Doctor."

The ugly man was impish.

If I wasn't allowed in, why was he just sitting there? Why didn't he do anything? Why didn't he say something?

I waited.

It was as if he forgot I was there.

"Forget it."

I followed the hedge down Madison to 55th. At the barbican an armed guard hailed me.

"Sir!"

"I'm here to see the Doctor."

"Sir!" the guard squinted.

"I have an appointment."

"I'm sorry, Sir?"

"I said I have an appointment."

"Let me ring the office," the guard ducked inside the barbican. Ringed by a row of Hemlock the ornately landscaped park fronted a flute shafted mansion with horseless carriages.

The guard popped out.

"I'm sorry, is this some kind of joke?"

"Some kind of joke? What are you talking about?"

"I'm sorry Sir," the guard stepped into the barbican. "Someone will escort you up directly."

"Thank you."

"Do you want to wait inside?"

"No. I'll only be here a moment."

"Sir?"

"I said I'll only be here a moment."

Burly guards with straight sticks donned the off-white garb of the institution, one clean shaven, the other with a long ropy beard.

The gate opened.

"For God sakes, I've been standing out here for an

eternity," I shouted.

"Sir?" the ropy bearded guard stammered.

"I said I've been out here for an eternity."

The guards looked at one another.

"Errrr, this way," the clean shaven guard pointed through the trees. The ropy bearded guard unlocked the front door of the mansion. We entered a narrow hallway just as a long case clock stuck the quarter hour. A woman with a yellow shawl sat at a typewriter. The shawl fell on the floor. She picked it up. As we climbed the staircase I got a look at her hands.

They were claws.

The guards escorted me to the end of the corridor.

"Come."

The clean shaven guard opened the door.

"We have a visitor, Sir."

"So far so good."

"Sir?"

"I might throw you a curve ball."

"Yes Sir!!"

I was ushered into a scholarly apartment expecting to see Doctor Maximilian Kilgore. The door closed and I found myself ensconced in Chesterfields, book cases, artifacts, and an alabaster bust. In a locked glass case was the red box.

"The red box."

I put my hands on the glass. The red box was an ultraviolet catastrophe, a schism riveting the dimensions of the room, the windowless chamber magnified a thousand fold, the source of the quantum interference, the sound of rain, the red box locked inside a simple glass case, if I could only get something to smash the glass.

"Looking for something?"

A Faustian figure in a brocade tailcoat pulled on a half bent taper. I was about to say something when the fog lifted and I could see down the valley.

Portland was gone.

"Look upon The City of Pain."

The Faustian figure thrust open the casement. A verdant forest stretched down the slope, columns of rain spilling as far as the eye could see.

"What happened," I gasped.

"Tell me. What do you see?"

I righted myself.

"Doctor Maximilian Kilgore."

"You know me?"

"I know you like I know myself."

Guilds Lake, Douglas Firs, Ponderosa Pines, a foundry of coal smokestacks, the Oregon Electric Railway line.

I was beginning to understand.

"Ogemtel," I said.

"Reversal is the first symptom."

"Symptom?"

"Repetition is the second. Super diseases, government treasons, foretelling future hotter seasons."

"What makes you think…"

"Think of mixing sinners with an protected soul, a defenseless true believer left to dig a deeper hole? And think to whom god hath bequeathed the role of slave and lord. How could a race of godless fakes keep Satan from its door? The sinners would invariably mix, a horror we could never fix, but if we move to seize the day, there might just be another way."

"Another way?"

"The afflicted, the sick of mind; a tortured soul isn't hard to find."

"I don't understand…"

"There are a billion people. The earth is full! A great war looms! A war to end all wars! Can you imagine what would happen if mankind doubled in size? Twice as many caches of sin? What would two great wars look like, then? And twice again? War all the time? Perpetual war? We must poison the weed of sin at its root! Cutting its stalks is not enough. Sever a branch, another checks its balance!"

"You are insane."

"Projection is the third symptom."

I swallowed painfully.

"My only goal is to control the hidden secret of the soul. In what pantopticon of pain remains arraigned inside the human brain a secret box that's tightly locked bred of sin and human shame?"

The Doctor gestured.

"Just look at yourself. You're afflicted. Sickness has taken hold. But luckily you have come to the right place. I am a Doctor. Fate is a bitter sister, ever since, no such thing as coincidence."

"No," I declared, "you don't understand."

"You've got it all backwards."

I backed out of the room. "Uh…do I make my own way out, Doctor?"

"They always say that, too."

"?"

"You can get him now."

The door opened.

"This man," the Doctor pined, "chimes like a chimera. He will stop at nothing to escape. Pay him no heed. He will try to convince you he is sane, and that it is you, in reality, who are mad."

"Yes, Doctor."

"Take him to Andrews. Prepare the operating theater. Then we may begin the…metaphysical" the Doctor cracked a rictus. "There is a new experiment I've been meaning to try, a rather grisly procedure I'm afraid, with negligible chance of success, but it seems fate has gifted you, gifted me, gifted us both with this opportunity."

"Yes, Doctor!"

The guards parlayed me downstairs. I went limp, picturing myself strapped to an operating table.

"Gentlemen, there must be some mistake! Look at me. I'm not crazy. I demand a phone call."

"Who are you going to call? Krazy Kat?"

The yellow shawl lie on the carpet. The woman carped,

gouged eye slits revealing putrescent orbs, a forked tongue lashing rotting teeth, claws rapping metal keys, the pendulum swinging back and forth.

"Gentlemen."

"You're mistaken."

"There's nothing gentle about us."

The guards eschewed me outside.

A red brick path led up the hill.

"Sirs, then. You've got to listen to me. I'm not crazy. The Doctor was referring to someone else."

"He was pointing at you."

"Sirs," I pursued, "don't hurt me."

"We won't."

"Now, what the Doctor does on his own, well, that's his business."

"Are you all mad?"

"I don't like this," the clean shaven guard said. "He's got a wild look in his eye."

We halted under the archivolt.

I could feel their grip loosening.

"What do we do?"

"I don't know."

In the downpour the archivolt afforded a glimpse of Northgate. A carriage passed by the interstice, driven by a man with a French Fork.

I sensed my opportunity.

"'Deep Sleep Theory,' remember?"

"Yeah, I remember. But I don't get it."

"You don't have to get it. You just have to do it."

"Right."

"Who are we to question? We do what we're told."

"You have free will," I interrupted. "Set me free. Let me go."

"All right. That's enough."

"Where are you taking me?"

"Doctor's orders."

"Please," I implored, "where are you taking me?"

The clean shaven guard chuckled.

"To a nice dry place."

"This is all a misunderstanding. A big mistake. I'm not crazy. I'm not who you think I am! I'm really someone else!"

"Now that's enough. The Doctor was right."

The guard's vice grip capitulated.

I was free.

"You'll fit in here nicely, madman."

Northgate was just across the pond. If I could scale the hedge I could return to the Mephistophelean House and the windowless chamber, back through the black X and pink circle. Before I could make it two steps a brawny arm hoisted me by the collar, brushing the stains off my pants.

"Now that's enough."

The guards escorted me up the hill. The Flemish gable of a refectory poked through the trees. A red brick path cut along the hedge and lead to a courtyard with Palladian windows. The clean shaven guard unlocked the door and we entered, shoulder to shoulder.

A man with pitted cheeks banged on the gate. The ropy bearded guard dragged him by the collar and whiplashed him into the backboard.

Teeth ricocheted across the floor.

I looked down.

There were a lot of teeth.

The gate opened.

A whale of an attendant took the man away.

The clean shaven guard confronted me.

"That's what you get for opening your mouth around here."

The guards escorted me to a gate where I was straight-jacketed and left half-sitting, half-leaning against the wall in a padded cell, a posterior restraint chained to a chord on the floor.

I waited. Having lost all circulation in my arms I concentrated on the window slit, fingers curling like rotting petals. Time was insignificant. I lost consciousness, only to awake minutes later thinking I had slept for hours. Finally the gate unlocked. The door opened. A hulking giant entered. On his belt was a ring of keys.

9 · Doctor Roland Andrews

"Ogemtel!"

"Have pity on me. What are you? Man or ghost?"

"Not man, though once I was. Let me go."

"Let you go?"

"Yes. Let me go."

"But why would I let you go?"

The hulking giant brown studied his placket front.

"I was the one that brought you here."

"You?"

"Name the man who's mad who doesn't think that he is sane who declares the dereliction of the melancholy brain. We call this place a mad house but we mean it makes men sane. Wouldn't that corrupt a world bent on that which one attains? What if what was, and the things that one does, turn out to be echoes of that which soon comes?"

"Ogemtel..."

"That is not my name."

"Who are you?"

"My name is Andrews."

"Doctor Roland Andrews?"

"Yes. Doctor Roland Andrews."

"Why did you say your name was Ogemtel?"

"The name of the curse, said in reverse, is all that I said to you."

"The curse," Ogemtel. O-G-E-M-T-E-L. TEL EM OG. LET-ME-GO.

Let me go.

"What's happening to me?"

The hulking giant glowered.

"What happened to Matthew? And Jonsrud? What did you do to my friends?"

"He's beginning to realize what I've done, what I had to do, to end this."

I cringed.

"If you speak out of turn, make amends or affirm an insidious quip or remark, it's your soul in a hole you'll be left to unfold and live out in a haze for the rest of your days."

"No..."

"Brain, tongue, teeth, feet, then left for dead at the side of the street. It's a daemon this Doctor, this Doctor a daemon, a pontifex preaching of Science, but careful unless you mistakenly lapse non-compliance or open defiance. He wants to cut out the erroneous people in order to build corrupt mercantile steeples, and all that remains of the children of sun will be lost in exhaust and forgot and undone."

"What do you want from me?"

The hulking giant was explicit.

"Take the executioner's mask and fit it on your face, end this madness lest he deign to doom the human race."

I closed my eyes. The padded floor was cement. The straightjacket was gone. The cell was gone. I lay on the floor of the windowless chamber under the black X and pink circle. I recognized the upside-down numbers on the wall. They repeated, over and over, every 174th line.

I blinked. For every event, past, present and future, there was an alternate outcome, a divergent reality that occupied the same space, the same water in the pond. Reality, a ripple in the pond where that which happened and all the things that didn't, awaited me on the other side of the black X and pink circle.

All I had to do was cast the stone.

"Shhhhzzzzz," the hulking giant harkened to the

window-slit.

Someone was standing outside.

"Follow me."

The hulking giant knocked on the door.

The cell opened.

The felt faced rube entered.

"This way."

Blood rushed to my head. The hulking giant escorted me to the gate. As the rube unclasped his key ring I snuck a peek inside the next cell.

It was Jonsrud.

"Ben?"

Jonsrud jumped to his feet.

"Is it you?"

"It's me."

"Are we in hell?"

"No."

"This is hell, isn't it?"

"No. Listen..."

"Ben, you've got to get me out of here. I failed the metaphysical. They're going to have to operate."

The hulking giant tapped my shoulder.

I whispered.

"Don't worry. I'll be back."

"This way," the rube reprimanded. I looked over my restraint.

Jonsrud pawed the window slit.

Was he right?

Were we in hell?

We crossed the exedra. Pandemonium broke out, bandages on shaven heads stained with blood and marking pens, men on gurneys, twins in chairs, dented heads with chopped off hair, screaming came from down the hall and touched off screaming from them all till white coats burst onto the scene and clubbed the screamers into dreams.

I kept my mouth shut.

The rube brandished his straight stick, cleaving a man's

jaw and hoisting him across his back. The twins circled the man with big ears fleeing the clutches of a whale. The hulking giant ushered me through the checkpoint down an anterior walkway back out in the storm.

It was raining so hard I had to shout.

"Who are those people?"

"Dullards. Cripples. Epileptics."

"You lock them up just because they're different?"

"They are wards of the State."

The red brick path linked the refectory to the building with Palladian windows. The asylum was a castle in a cloud, quoins and tourelles, double pitched roofs with gabled dormers, copper hips and iron cresting, eyelid garrets and corbeled gambrel.

"Where are you taking me?"

"They have to believe I'm taking you to the Bolgia."

We walked brusquely. The straight jacket cut into my skin like a drowning sack. Runoff spilled from the pent roof of the refectory, fog swallowing the asylum in a cauldron of mist. The broad slope swelled, the brick path welted in phantasms. Adjacent the hedge I could see Northgate. In my straightjacket I could cause a disturbance at the turnstile, but with no way to operate the controls, I had no way out.

What if I did escape?

What if I returned to the Mephisthophelean House?

A high wall was barbed in wire coping. We followed the red brick path to a little door between the refectory and hedge. The hulking giant unlocked the door and pointed to a boiler room.

"It's safe to talk here."

Rolled plate boilers roiled wrought iron vents. High pressure steam fueled fulsome sulfur jets. There was a cot, locker, and mirror. The hulking giant sank on the cot, looking like a man possessed.

"Now is the time. We must strike before he is the wiser. Although he is beginning to piece it together, he does not recognize you. I'll expedite you to the Bolgia in a rigged jacket. It is our only chance. Once he's gone, we can get the key."

"The key?"

"To the red box."

"The red box?"

"Don't concern yourself with the red box. Remember, he is a tempter. He is not to be trusted, even for an instant. He will tempt you with the red box. It is the source of his power. Do not look inside, even for an instant."

"The source of his power?"

Quantum interference issued from the very same red box I had seen in the Doctor's study and the windowless chamber. It was the source of the nadir.

And my absolution.

"What's in the red box?"

"A cathexis. It is like a mirror. Once you look into it, you see things as they really are."

"What do I do?"

I hesitated, trying to envision myself strapped to the Doctor's operating table.

The hulking giant drew to his full height. "The scourge of man, he works alone inside the Operating Theatre. Wait until he turns his back. Then strike. Be careful, though. Don't listen to what he says. In devils haven you must sojourn, lock the door, and make him burn."

"How can I trust you?"

"How can you trust yourself?"

The mirror hung on the wall.

The straightjacket dripped on the floor.

"Take off the restraint."

The hulking giant was right.

How could I trust myself?

"There are nine wards here at the House on the Hill, nine levels of hell just to face him still. A forest of sand and a skeleton key unlocks the box to the Weeping Tree."

"The Weeping Tree…"

"But if you listen to the lies that he will tell about

himself, you will wake up in a dream believing you're somebody else. Do not listen to the things he says, pay his words no heed, for your parts won't fit together and your eyes'll start to bleed."

"What if I can't ignore him?"

"Trust me."

"What will happen?"

"You will leave with less than you came."

I peered at my reflection in a pond, stone in hand.

"Once inside the inner chamber you will face a greater danger. Through the center you must pass to step inside the looking glass. Things will all be upside-down, bones of traitors on the ground, and he'll be there alight on wings, the witch doctor, the fallen king."

"What must I do?"

"Do what you must."

The hulking giant unfastened the restraint.

The straightjacket fell on the floor.

"Jonsrud's here."

The hulking giant stepped back.

"Your other friend's here, too."

"Matthew?"

The hulking giant nodded.

"Give me your keys."

"Keys? Yes. Hmmmmnnzzzzzzz. There are a lot of doors that need locking…"

"How can I free my friends?"

"First the Doctor. Then your friends."

"No."

"You don't get it, do you? Have you looked at yourself? There. Look," the hulking giant pointed at the mirror.

"What do you mean?"

"Look!"

I seized the hulking giant by the shoulders.

"Help me!"

"The Doctor keeps the key inside his cursed locked red box, but if you want to take it from him be the one that he forgot."

"But you've got to help me!"

"You've got to go, you've got to try, you've got to take him out, pretty soon a weaker fever starts to set you out, you may try to run away but in the end you'll be found out, for the Doctor never lingers over those who would cast doubt."

"Why don't you help me?"

"What you don't know can't hurt you."

"What don't I know?"

The hulking giant pulled a straightjacket from the locker and a bottle from his pocket. "Take this laudanum. I'll expedite you to the Bolgia. You will not be forced to dwell upon the misfortunes of others although you'll hear grisly screaming from ancient ghosts howling over their second death. The Doctor paints in pain. Look," the hulking giant peeled the restraint, "the arm-locks have reverse catches. You can free yourself with a flick of your wrist. We'll try it out before we go."

"Tell me what you know."

"The Doctor and I went to school together. I was the pessimist. He, the optimist. I set out to prove what I believed. He set out to believe what he proved. Somehow, over time, our roles reversed. We meant to meet up in the middle, but ended up going our own way."

"What difference does it make?"

"One day I looked into the mirror and beheld that which I feared."

"What difference does it make?"

"For that which I feared possessed me. I saw It in the mirror. It was always there. To be conscious of It is to be cursed by consciousness. Free will is not an illusion. Free will takes over your life. You dream you are free. But you are not. Free of dreams you are not free at all. Free will is a paradox. Call it what you will. To Hell we must him send, or else this day will never end, things will always stay the same, it will never cease to rain."

And the hulking giant, Roland Andrews, pointed to the

clock on the locker.

"When did you arrive?"

"I don't know."

"Has night come?"

I rubbed my eyes.

I couldn't believe it was day.

"And do you not grow fatigued?"

"Yes."

"There's only one left, now."

"One?"

"One of 174."

"174?"

"The last piece in the puzzle. The only thing standing in his way. One missing piece. 1 of 174."

The hulking giant offered the straightjacket.

An icy twinge mid-lined my gut, the hulking giant's face splintering in boils, eyes rolling back in his head, the boiler room bursting open, a cacophony of lightning and thunder.

"Number 174.....number 174, have you found what it is you were looking for?"

"What do you mean, number 174?"

"Do you abhor, number 174, what it is, you'll be made to account for?"

"What can I do?" I screamed.

"A surgeon's knot, a secret plot, involving X which marks the spot, a hangman's noose tied too loose by hands he used and then forgot."

The peeling wall.

The cot.

The mirror.

"Number 174, Number 174, are you sorry for the things that you left on the floor?"

"Things? What things?"

The broiler.

The laudanum.

The straightjacket.

"What did *I* do?"

Pebbles of hail bounced on the goblin-green grass, grape stumps, fern wedges, sitka and laurel, tanoaks with star shaped piths disemboguing an invulnerable wall of thorns. The red brick path was dirgelike through the careworn, waxy trees.

"What reason do I have not to trust him? He could have just as easily delivered me to the Doctor. It doesn't make any sense."

I looked down.

There was blood on the grass.

"If I can find a way over the fence we can make a break for the House, back to the windowless chamber."

I followed the hedge. There was a bosk next to the refectory. I scanned the grounds like a madman breaking in for some inane reason to very same asylum he was escaping from. White caps jutted across the gust front, squall line cleated in bands, the branch strokes of an anvil crawler pleating the vort lobe.

The refectory door opened. Two men in white coats kicked up fields of rubicund flecks, spotting their coattails and ties.

I dove behind the archivolt.

The footsteps circled.

Rain fell in sheets. I brought my hands to my face. I had to get out of the storm. Water gushed off the cooper roof of a chapel. A pipe organ played softly. Stained glass windows depicted a lonely figure assailed by beasts.

A concussion throttled the viaduct.

My outline was inflamed.

I looked through the trees.

All was still.

Nothing stirred.

A deluge erupted. The buildings at the end of the copse faded, rivulets forming fast flowing streams. The white coats disappeared inside the building with Palladian windows. I abandoned the archivolt and gamboled over the embankment, falling face first in a pond.

Lightning struck.

The water was electric.

My pulse coruscated.

"Oh god..."

I scrambled to my knees and ran down the brick path. Northgate was adjacent the chapel. I approached the guard-house and looked inside.

The ugly man sat on the stool.

I knocked.

Nothing happened.

I rattled the bars.

The guardhouse remained under lock and key.

"How am I going to get out?"

There was no way over the fence.

"I have to find another way."

A three story annex with transom fanlights and mulled windows overlooked Madison Avenue. I noticed a gap between the foundation and fence permitting access to a crawlspace, the water-poked boughs of the hedge tinseled in razor wire. I cleaved the thorns, hoping to find a weakness, barbed halos like rain-glossed spider webs.

The crawlspace opened up and I found myself able to stand. I searched for a sturdy foothold and hoisted myself up the pleaching. The branches thinned out, revealing the upper floors of the annex.

The silhouette of a man stood in a third story window.

It was Matthew.

"Matthew?"

I could not tell if he saw me.

"Ah!" I pricked my finger. Pain shot up my arm. I stuck my finger in my mouth. My tongue constricted.

"What the…"

I hallucinated. The hedge was melting. Thorns barbed my knuckles and embedded in my bones. The hedge appeared to shear into the downpour and the loam. I shimmied on the V-shaped post where sleeve and ring were split, a man-sized hole just big enough through which someone could fit.

"There is a way out!"

I tested the footing.

It was solid.

I hesitated.

"What if that which grants salvation guarantees annihilation?"

From far away I heard a scream.

The hole in the fence teetered in the wind.

10 · Elysian Fields

My finger discolored. A necrotic paralysis anesthetized my extremities. Viscous fluid bubbled down my chin. I touched my face.

My eyes were bleeding.

I poked my way back through the thorns, rubbing my shoulder in agony. The wind sheared the crawlspace. Thorns scuffed my jacket like poisoned plantains. I emerged from the hedge and climbed annex steps.

There was a sign on the rivulet.

Elysian Fields
'lasciate ogni speranza, voi ch'entrate'

I tested the entryway. It was unsecured. An enameled fresco depicted forests, castles and lakes. A knotted pile carpet reeked of ether and nitrous oxide. At the end of a hall was a stairwell, doors on both sides.

I heard voices.

A door opened.

A nurse appeared.

I pressed against the wall.

How could I have gone unnoticed?

Surely the nurse had seen me.

I peeked around the corner. The nurse unlocked a utility closet, filling a bucket with water. I hastened noiselessly, the green carpet eating my footsteps.

"…dirty as the dead…dirty as the dead…you'll see what I mean when you're dirty as the dead…"

I headed upstairs. The third floor was unattended. A cell midway down the hall had a chair, a bed and a table. The hedge was visible through the window.

I opened the next door.

It had the same view.

I checked the next cell.

And the next.

They were all the same.

"If the House on the Hill is a paradox, a reality onto itself, wouldn't the outer wall really be the inner wall? Regardless of the view outside?"

I fingered the median door on the inner wall, fumbling in the dark for the light switch.

"Matthew?"

Matthew sat up in bed.

"It's me! Let's go. We're getting out here!"

Matthew got out of bed.

A blank spot besmirched the bedcover.

"It's not so bad here. Places are the same. People, too. Just arranged differently. There are voices upstairs. There are voices downstairs. But it doesn't matter. They're there, and I'm here. To tell you the truth, I like it when they lock the door. Keeps the crazies out."

"But the door isn't locked! Only in your mind are you imprisoned. Quick. We don't have time. We're getting out."

"I'm not leaving," Matthew said.

"Escape is no farther than your window. Look! Can't you see? There's a hole in the fence. I know the way back, back through the black X and pink circle."

"It's no use. You'll end up where you started. All places are the same. People too. Just arranged differently."

"Look. If you won't come, at least point me to the Doctor."

"You want me to take you to…Him?"

"Yes."

"He's a lot like you, you know…just arranged differently."

"Where is he?"

Could I trust him? Could I trust him not to betray me? Everything seemed hackneyed.

A staged event.

"Jonsrud. We have to get Jonsrud. He's here, in the building with Palladian windows."

"Menos Hall."

"Let's go to Menos Hall."

"No."

"Why not?" I cried.

"We'll be caught. If were caught, we'll be put in the hole."

"The hole?"

Matthew scratched the blank spot.

"I'm staying here."

"Staying here? Are you crazy? If you don't come with me, save yourself."

Matthew melted from my grasp.

"Don't you want to save yourself?"

"There is no salvation."

Before I could catch him he was through the door and down the hall.

"Matthew," I yelled, pursuing muffled footsteps down the green carpet.

"Matthew!"

The door swung on the hinge.

Matthew was gone.

"Matthew!"

The door creaked. The nurse was gone. I slunk across the carpet fixated on the muffled voices down the hall, knowing that at any instant the door might open and there would be nowhere to hide. Luckily the door did not open and I traversed Elysian Fields undetected.

Horsetail and sitka sledge moated cinders, toad rush, and ash. I stood ankle deep in the mud, my disappointment

ebbing. In losing Mathew I lost nothing.
    "Jonsrud."

11 · Menos Hall

The turnstile torqued like a man catcher. Northgate was a roping shoot. The gabled roofs and archways were bedizened in the lightning. From my vantage point I could see the red brick path leading through the trees to the building with Palladian windows. Beyond the refectory the red brick path terminated in the courtyard. A drain gurgled next to a rock pile. Pine cones floated in a can. A placard read,

Menos Hall

"Menos Hall. This is it."

The rocks in the pile were full of holes. I took the biggest one I could find and pressed the courtyard door, the fear of getting caught replaying itself over and over.

What if my timing was off?

What if I ran into someone?

I tiptoed upstairs. There was a judas hole. I looked inside. The felt faced rube leaned against the gate.

"Just what the Doctor ordered."

I pressed the door.

The hinges creaked.

The felt faced rube did not stir.

I doubted myself.

Could I go on?

The burnished door swung noiselessly ajar.

Water dripped from my clothes. The felt faced rube must have been asleep for he remained in his chair.

I crept up behind him.

The rube opened his eyes.

"Hey."

I smashed the rock in his eye.

"You're going to pay for that."

A roughshod roundhouse cracked his temple.

The rube fell on the floor.

"Erhh."

I discarded the rock, took the straight stick, and found a set of keys in his pocket. Tubing his appendages in a straightjacket I dug my foot in his back, looped the bracers, and secured the restraint.

"Surprised I knew how to do that."

The rube bled on the floor.

"Shouldn't sleep on the job."

Jonsrud was nowhere to be seen.

I dragged the rube in a cell.

"What the, hey, what!?"

I hogtied the double bracer to the posterior restraint and leaned against the wall.

"Bu....Wh...Wha......Why? What did I do? What did I do?"

I didn't know what to say.

No one would hear his cries.

I double checked the outer cells, certain Jonsrud was there. All were occupied by the unfortunate wards of the House on Asylum Road, umbrageous, recondite, rueful, with eyes that hung from their sockets. The cell in which I remembered Jonsrud to be was unoccupied.

The bars of the iron gate blocked access to the inner ward. I unlocked the gate and looked inside.

Jonsrud was gone.

The rube whimpered.

I drew the straight stick.

"You know what," I reminisced, "this is the same cell I

was in, isn't it."

"I just did what I was told."

"The cell **you** put me in."

The straight stick pivoted.

"Please. Don't."

"Where is the blonde man with long hair who was housed here?"

"Wh...wh...wh...what?"

I scoffed.

"Where is Jonsrud?"

The rube feigned.

"Is it me or is everyone here crazy? Jonsrud. The blond man with blue eyes and long hair? Where did you take him, you bastard?"

"To...to...to...to... but...but...but..."

"But what?"

"But...I...I...just...did what I was told..."

"Where is he?"

"I...I...I...I did what I was told, oh Lord, I did what I was told, I did what I was told, oh Lord, don't put me in the hole."

"Speak up, you loony."

"Don't put me in the hole again, don't put me in the hole. I beg you on my mortal soul, don't put me in the hole. I did what I was told, oh Lord, I did what I was told, I did what I was told, oh Lord, don't put me in the hole."

"Tell me where he is or I'll..."

"He's...he's..mma...he's in...he's in...mma"

"Spit it out, fat boy," the straight stick tapped his temple.

"Mma, mmm, mmale, Malebolge Manor, The Operating Theater...but I did what I was told, oh lord, don't put me in the hole...I beg you on my mortal soul, don't put me in the hole..."

I left him in the cell. Sensation returned to my extremities, the sensation of pain. I made my way back to the courtyard, straight stick in my hand, keys in my pocket, rain in the courtyard.

"I feel a sickness in my soul take hold and start to spread, what tortures are awaiting me, what travesties, what dread, what alternate reality is this through which I tread, eternal life bequeathed the dead, what secrets hide within my head, which secrets better left unsaid?"

There was a high wall running from Menos Hall to an iron promontory. I exited the courtyard trusting in the imperative for self-preservation. There was no one in sight. I followed the wall up the path. A portcullis with a grip hoist joined the promontory to the hedge. A key from the rube's ring penetrated the lock. The portcullis retracted.

It was bedlam. A knot garden was immured in thunder and lightning. A man ran in a boot of nails, men wrestled in a pit, a hip faced girl hid in the hedge beneath a pruned soffit. The tortured souls stripped to the waist sought shelter from the storm, but there was nowhere to hide inside a warren of dolor.

A guard appeared in a tower. I cornered the gangway unchallenged, keeping out of sight. An attendant stepped from the trees, blocking my way.

I clutched the straight stick.

The attendant shunted the gangway.

How could I have gone unnoticed?

Was I a ghost?

A non-entity?

"They must think I'm one of them."

Metal spiders ran down my spine. I ripped a thorn out of my shoulder and looked at it.

It was barbed, like a flail.

"This place is a torture factory."

I heard screaming. I snuck under the gangway and followed the hedge, coming to a copse. A man climbed a trellis of thorns pursued by a gristly hound. Thorns ribboned the poor man's hands, the hound pulling him down. Feathers of flesh as it clamped and it jerked and reworked the man's bleeding leg stumps matted the fur of the bullheaded cur with his offal, his man-hash, and lumps. A sneering attendant looked on in delight as he fed the hound more and more chain, biting and clawing it's way up the trellis he gave the hound complete free reign.

Clouds swallowed the trees, the grounds a marshy mire, a metallic lockstep under thunder tripping through the wire. I pressed against the hedge and turned to face that which I feared, the noxious spit and stinking breath of ludic whispering in my ear.

"They locked me in a boot of nails, bolted to my bones, and force me till I've had my fill, a stomach full of stones."

The booted man then let me go and cried out in despair, clanking ankle deep in mud began to pull out all his hair. In his wake I saw a break hewn in the hedge a flight of stairs, a columned concourse overlooking the inimical parterre. Thunder bled and lightning scoured alternating shadows, and I pitied the abandoned souls cast out and left to harrow, jabbed in guts and sucker punched with straight sticks snapped across their knees, the tortured souls left to succumb to an insane hierarchy.

I had a change of heart.

"Each and every tortured soul, a victim of the State's control, an offshoot culled to stave the whole, it's time to give back what you stole."

A column with scrolls and acanthus leaves bore the inscription,

Malebolge Manor

12 · Malebolge Manor

"Jonsrud."

I tried to get my bearings. A field of capitals bracketed a stylobate. The field was constructed with such mathematical precision that every direction terminated in a colonnade. I projected a solid line through the columns, careful not to lose myself in the illusion.

Lightning arrayed. Wind hit my face. I wondered if I was coming to the center. To my surprise I found myself back over the parterre. Unable to judge direction, I returned to the very same spot from which I began.

The journey was catching up with me. I was horrified by the prospect that I might become one of the tortured souls in the yard, stripped to the waist in the thunder and lightning. I reengaged the field but every direction looked the same. There was no way through.

I picked a piece of slate off the concourse and marked the entasis of the outer column, stepping across the grid to the next. I repeated the process, thereby marking each entasis. Column by column I vectored the field in what I reasoned a straight line to be.

The rain quickened. The wind blew in my face. I stepped out onto the columned concourse.

A roving attendant took out his straight stick and unloosed on those sinking into the pit. The sneering attendant emerged from the copse, the gristly hound foaming and licking its chops. A man in the pit fought to pull himself up and ran into the copse with his tongue sticking out. The sneering attendant then let loose the chain, from the copse came the sound of the screaming again.

I faced the colonnade.

"If everything's upside-down, would a straight line really be straight? Wouldn't it curve? Into a circle? Wouldn't a straight line curve into a perfect circle?"

The hash marks projected a theoretical line. I veered, expecting to find myself back on the concourse, but to my astonishment the rain faded and vapor collected on the stones.

"This is it."

Columns jutted like deadwood. I continued, going nowhere, looping around and around, losing sight of the hash marks. I noticed a discoloration in the distance. A wall with no doors stretched uniformly into a ruined field.

"A wall. But no way around."

I heard footsteps.

A shadow crossed the colonnade.

The footsteps halted.

I gripped the straight stick. My breath misted. From behind the entasis I could hear breathing. Vapor sluiced like slurry. The wall stretched in both directions, staid columns a broken field of monoliths.

The straight stick descanted.

The vapor coalesced.

The footsteps receded.

The shadow split the mire.

I exhaled.

"How long until my luck runs out?"

I trailed the footsteps through the columns, keeping my distance, but the shadow gave pause and I began to second guess myself.

"This is too easy."

In the stony field I could hear perfectly. A key was inserted in a lock. A door opened. The door shut. The footsteps were gone.

I peeked from behind a shaft.

A blivet was vaulted in a recess.

"Menos Hall."

I grasped the blivet.

It seared like a devil's fork.

"I hope I have the right key."

I began feeding keys into a mortise lock. Heat from the wall radiated across the bridge of my nose. The metal surface glowed. I was running out of keys. Several I had used; of the few that remained, only one fit.

The mortise released the blivet.

The door opened.

Luciferin effused a hellish painting upon an ambulatory wall. A city caught fire, lit coals fell from the sky, burning bodies in boiling rivers, the vanquished clawing their way from immolation only to be quartered by blade wielding daemons who appeared to be the very same overlords inciting battle in the first place.

The longer I looked at the painting, the more cracks appeared. The columns in the ruined field were in the library. The gargoyles on the old dorm block were pigeons in the tree.

There were two doors. One was a storage closet. The other was a checkpoint.

Guards played cards on a metal folding table.

"Hey, did you hear something?"

The door shut.

I backtracked through the ambulatory and hid in the storage closet.

I could hear footsteps.

My breathing slowed. I cleared my mind, gripping the straight stick.

The closet opened.

Light spilled on the floor.

'Don't turn the light on.'

The door shut. I could hear voices.

Had I been discovered?

Somebody laughed.

A match struck.

The ironclad door gnashed shut.

Menos Hall was silent.

The ambulatory was empty. I infiltrated the checkpoint and operated the lever to the gate. To my disdain I found yet another locked door. I withdrew the ring, wondering how much time I'd have before the guards returned.

What if I didn't have the right key?

One by one the keys didn't work.

Down the corridor I could hear the mortise lock.

The ironclad door opened.

The guards were returning.

I dropped the keys.

"No!"

Before I knew it I had snatched the ring off the floor and inserted another key. The lock unbolted and I stepped onto a cellblock, slamming the door behind me.

It was as hot as hell. A maniacal ensemble of despondency and despair cased holding pens like animals in cages, alerting one another to my presence.

It was as if they were expecting me.

"Heretic, Heretic!"

"My eyes! My eyes!"

"What I wouldn't give to meet you face to face!"

To cross the module I had to pass through the holding pens. Each pen had a chuck hole, vestibule, and flume. I passed the first pen. Instinctually I stepped back, and not an instant too soon, for two arms shot through the bars and wrapped around my neck.

I fell backwards.

"Almost got you, Doc."

"Doc," I choked. "Me?"

"Of course your honor."

An albino with tattooed jowls cracked his knuckles.

"You mistake me for someone else."

"You're an infernal bastard but I love you none the

less. Listen Doc. You got to let me go. I'm on your side. You were right. Everyone here *is* nuts."

"I'm trapped here, just like you."

The albino jeered.

"Come on Doc. Give me a shot before you put me in the hole."

"Let me alone."

"Leaving well enough alone lent itself well enough. I'm a dissenter."

"Let me pass."

"One shot is all I ask. Bring one up from the hotel. We can have some fun. Some good, clean fun."

I left the albino in the pen. Fungused fingernails tapped the bars of the next pen.

"Afternoon, Governor."

I shivered.

Jackleg forearms collared the chuck hole.

"Purple Face and I we're wondering if you could settle an argument."

"I'm sorry, I…"

"Don't walk out on me," the forearms lunged.

I jumped.

"Didn't mean to be antisocial, Gov. I can barely control myself. It's a sign of the times. A sign of the times. Reason with me Gov. If each person is a product of their environment, why am I held responsible for that which the environment produced? Am I on trial?"

"Here," I vouchsafed, "we are all on trial."

"I guess that makes you judge, jury, and executioner."

I flinched, and not a moment too soon.

I was missing a piece of my hair.

"Purple Face and I have our disagreements, but there's one thing we can agree on."

"You are mistaken. I'm not who you think I am."

"If Purple Face is a product of his environment, is it fair to condemn him for what he will become?"

"What's that smell?"

In the adjoining pen a figure sat in a chair. The figure didn't move.

A fullered seax lay at its feet.

The ash was streaked in crimson.

"Oh my god."

"You could say I talked him into it. But he didn't need much convincing. Good old Purple Face, a sign of the times, Gov, a sign of the times. The thing I want to know is, if Purple Face really is a product of his environment, why is he being held responsible for factors beyond his control?"

I was sick.

"A sign of the times, a sing of the times. Might be tempted to do it myself. Mind you he knew what crimes he was committing. We're all guilty of something. No one is without sin. Look at how he displeases himself in his own image. A crime against nature, for what criminals are worth, a dime a dozen I daresay, consider yourself, Governor, locking me in this cell, next to Purple Face, you maniacal, bloody bastard!"

"You've got it all wrong," I pleaded, "you mistake me for someone else."

"Purple Face and I are Devil's Advocate. For us there is no common ground. He says one thing, I say another. He'd say I'm upside down, I'd say he's inside out."

Flies buzzed. The heat was incapacitating. The odor of purification made me wretch. A pale spot of light illuminated the next pen. A man was bolted to the wall.

I seized the bars.

"Can you hear me?"

The figure twitched.

"He'd say I'm up in arms, I'd say he's checked out. He'd say I'm spinning yarns, I'd say it's in doubt. But there was one thing, one thing, Purple Face and I could always agree upon. Know what it is?"

Jonsrud wasn't anywhere. The cellblock ended and I came to another locked door.

"Take a guess, Gov."

I looked over my shoulder.

"He said you'll pay for what you've done."

A key from the ring unbolted the door to a Penrose staircase. A sign was affixed to some bricks in the wall that were moldered and had been replaced.

F3	Administration
F2	Records
F1	**Holding Cells**
B1	Bolgia 1-10
B2	Operating Theatre

"The Operating Theatre. That's it."

A knob shot off a radiator, hitting me in the face.

"Damnation!"

The knob clattered down the staircase.

Tungsten jets cast an uneven, sickly glow over the corkscrewing steps. I tried to keep pace but my feet were too big. The risers were pitted in knots and cavities cut in the mineral rift, the olivine wedges and quartz framework grains receding back into the cliff. Newel posts cast toxic shadows across the sandstone wall; I lost my footing on the tread and began to slip and fall.

"Argh."

Vortex streets and strange attractors blocked the long descent, a conic helix winding down the deeper that I went. After what seemed an eternity of paradox and peril, a lancet door was reinforced and hewn into a carrel.

F3	Administration
F2	Records
F1	Holding Cells
B1	**Bolgia 1-10**
B2	Operating Theatre

"This must be the way to the Operating Theatre."

I inspected the ring.

"The key to the gate, the key to the cell, the portcullis, blivet and post. How many keys have I used? How many remain?"

One by one the keys were unsuccessful.

I inserted the second to last key.

The lock engaged.

The door opened.

I had a terrifying thought.

Door after door, lock after lock, the keys spun around the ring. But one key remained. I could unlock one more door. What if I used all my keys and came to a door I couldn't unlock, having penetrated the perfect prison, only to find myself locked inside?

13 · The Bolgia

Ten pens, numbered one to ten, decocted a zoo of the irredeemable, tourniquets of torture, contraptions of debasement, widgets of grief and despair, jiggers of hopelessness, anguish, and throe sweltering in charcoal air. Like ditches of stone that were splintered in bone the Bolgia were blighted and bare, the interred locked inside left to claw out their eyes while reciting in vain the Lord's Prayer. Arches and dikes of livid stone projected a field malign, an iron well and a bottomless pit demarcated a strike-slip line.

In the first Bolgia, eyes cast down, were wielders of the lash, caching perfect human forms into the gall-flecked fetid ash. Inside Bolgia two a man was buried in ordure, a stream of falsely metered words recurred an addlepated curse. Bolgia three was breamed in screams, a man housed in a block, his soles poked holes in beds of coals, his knees cut on the rock. He leaned against the block to cut the pressure on his spine, but fell back onto the hot coals screaming each and every time.

I rattled the bars.

It was no use.

There was no way out.

"I have to find Jonsrud."

A form distorted chin to chest inside Bolgia four had a torso wholly turned awry with eyes that blinked no more. So dark it was I barely saw the outline of his face, disconnected from his body and then put back in its place. The shoulders arched grotesquely forward, body in a brace, the inverted torso's sunken sockets staring into space.

"How has he done it, what purpose does it serve, to break a man in two, only to set him in reverse?"

I pitied the multitude. Unable to quell my lingering suspicions I foresaw Jonsrud bound in some similar, inconceivable deprivation.

Bolgia five was limed in pitch and red hot grappling-irons, an unctuous wight of lofty height was wrapped in metal wires.

"I know it's my turn to burn in the urn, but explain this to me this, my one final concern."

"Final concern?"

"Why do I belong next to him?"

He pointed to the face-backwards thing.

"Don't ask me about the logic of this place!"

"Don't you know who I am? I am the one who cleared the land and brought you here in my name. I buried the stories that you told your babies, replaced your old laws with laws of my own. The words that you used are all lost and forgotten like fruit in a tree that's already rotten, the eye on the pyramid belongs to me, and the bones in the base are what you will be."

I pressed the ring against my belt.

"Open the door. Let-me-go!"

I did not pity the soul inside Bolgia five.

Bolgia six was empty. Bolgia seven housed victims of botched surgeries, amputations, collections of missing parts. Bolgia eight housed by all appearances someone who should not have been there.

I reached through the bars.

"What is the reason for your internment?"

"I don't know why I'm here, though I tried to be God to myself. I persisted in trying to make my own way, but got stuck on the hook when I went for the bait."

The heat was atramentous.

"Where am I headed next?"

Bitterly I asked myself.

"I am lost."

"We are all lost."

A prostrate form lay on the floor inside Bolgia nine. Cuts and scars and strange burn marks ran up and down his spine. Bolgia ten was another double pen, a man lashed to a rack. A torturess in surgical dress drew black lines down his back. The short hand of the torturess was delicate and merciless, inscribing sharp-tongued smoking steel filleting strips across his chest.

My momentum expired.

I could go no farther.

The torturess japed.

Bolgia ten opened.

I must go on, I told myself.

I must go on.

A mutilated keyway was fixed under a louvered track.

One key remained.

I had come to my destination.

I fit the final key in the lock.

The door opened onto an antediluvian blastway, arcs of heat radiating into the throat of the cone. A chilled, ice tempered expanse was devoid of sound and color, moonmilk and frostwork glinting like jewels on a rimstone dam. Unsure of my footing I skirted the chasm, erasing the momentum of fear building up inside me. The freezing gallery narrowed and I found myself at a dead end. A familiar impression was fixed upon the gallery wall.

F3	Administration
F2	Records
F1	Holding Cells
B1	Bolgia 1-10
B2	**Operating Theatre**

Jonsrud lay on the table.

He was still.

A blood spackled garment hung on the wall.

"What has he done to you?"

There was a scalpel on the tray.

I picked it up.

"An eye for an eye, a soul for a soul, a part of the whole with a heart of coal."

"And what would you know of the human soul," Doctor Maximilian Kilgore threw a saw in the sink.

"Doctor Maximilian Kilgore."

The Doctor took off his gloves.

"You look lost."

"I seem to have found my way here."

"You certainly have."

"Have I caught you at a bad time?"

"Not at all. And to think, I had the whole place on the lookout, a man on the run, and here you were, all along."

The Doctor pointed to the gallery.

"Shall we?"

"Of course."

"This way."

I followed the Doctor. Although he preceded, he had a way of looking behind his shoulder.

'A useful skill.'

The Doctor drew a flowstone curtain.

"Where does it lead?"

I had the distinct impression the Doctor could read my thoughts.

"The surgery here at the House on the Hill has failure and success, finding what is good in man is an eternal game of chess. A bibliography containing all that's good and bad is exactly what's required to redeem those who are mad. A day will come when what we do will be on a grand scale, a logarithmic multitude, a brand new holy grail. Compendiums of that which happened and that which did not, will awaken what's forsaken in the lies you have been taught. From the tiniest quirk to the man gone berserk, we've begun to unwind the mind's pagan clockwork. At which point does vision come too spliced to see? Do we get what we came for? Do we unearth the key?"

"After you."

"Of course."

The flowstone curtain revealed a flight of stairs. As we climbed I laid hold of the scalpel. The Doctor was saying something but I didn't pay attention. I could feel quantum interference. Far above a particle of light pierced the gloom, a jewel atop a ladder of thorns. The Doctor pointed to an acropolis. A door opened. Thunder and rain hammered the casement. Tulip glass shades and brown leather chaises adjoined a mahogany breakfront. Pembroke tables with lacquered drop-leafs, Chesterfields with studded rings, the locked glass case and alabaster bust, red box in its center.

The Doctor opened a folding bar.

"May I offer you some respite?"

"Of what?"

"Rotgut."

"Rotgut?"

"It means, 'good red.'"

The Doctor extended a glass.

"To your health," the Doctor offered.

"Yes. To my health."

I drank to my health.

I could not say what the Doctor drank to.

"You think I poison you?"

"The thought had crossed my mind."

The Doctor took the glass.

"You've seen what we do here?"

"I've seen enough."

"You haven't seen anything yet."

The Doctor set the glasses on the drop-leaf. My gaze shifted to the case. Quantum interference rent a schism in the dimensions of the room. The red box irradiated a cross polarized field, base caps over crown molding, the ceiling inside out, everything in two places at once. I could feel the Doctor's stare on the back of my neck.

"What's inside the red box?"

"The red box?"

"The red box, Doc, the red box. What's inside the red box?"

"The red box, like you and me, is a probability calculated in a field."

"That's all you've got?"

"When you witness an event, does not being there in and of itself alter the conditions of that which occurred?"

I couldn't take my eyes off the red box.

The Doctor's words were narcotic.

"In a time when the sane seem mad and mad seem sane, it falls on us to prescribe the blame."

Rain pattered the casement. My stomach congealed. The Rotgut was a pool of ambrosia, the Doctor's teeth, grinder blades.

"The red box, the red box," the Doctor contemplated, "what's inside the red box? A piece of the hole inside your soul you've found by yourself that you can't control. Narcissus nevermore, may I implore, what it is, that you thought, that you came for?"

I dehisced.

Corpuscles clouded, fanned by unseen wings.

"Call me an Opportunist."

"An Opportunist?"

"Yes. And what do you call yourself?"

I winced.

What could I share?

When should I lie?

I had to get my hands on the red box.

"The red box, Doc, the red box. You were getting to the red box."

The Doctor stretched the height of the chamber unfurling gigantic wings, a phantasm hovering above my head inside the corpuscle cloud.

"Wish to glance inside the glass, to look no more, but know at last, the true form you've been undermining, masking, hiding, coinciding?"

"You speak in riddles, Doctor. I have seen your nine wards. You lord like a fallen angel over a frozen sea."

"Do you know yourself like you know your fellow man? Are you aware of the human condition? What awaits you when you die, on the other side? Could you say with any certainty what sort of man you were? How would you pass judgment on yourself?"

The scalpel slipped.

"Don't you want to know? Don't you want to splice in time, see what things its shows? Don't you want to take a chance and glance inside my looking glass? Just once, to see yourself, as you really are?"

"The mirror?"

"For the first time."

I had to chance it.

I had to look inside the red box.

"What sort of hell have you created?"

"Isn't there a piece of hell that's hidden in us all, a number stamp marked on your soul that you can't uninstall? A unique number branded and encoded on your being and you're left to wander purgatory looking for its meaning. God's cow, bag of bones, guts are made of sticks and stones, a piece of offal granted life you yearn for peace but live in strife. Clueless what it's all about you realize there's no way out. You're trapped inside an empty shell that's nothing more than organelles and just too late you comprehend you're nothing more than odds and ends."

"There is such a thing as free will."

"Free will is a metaphysical dilemma. There is no reality outside of language. When we destroy something, we do not just destroy it. We create its opposite. The world is not what we've destroyed, but that which fills the void. Is it not the same in the soul of man? Would not the destruction of consciousness absolve that which it haunts, creating its opposite?"

"The opposite of what?"

"Original sin."

"Original sin?"

"To look inside the looking glass is to see yourself as you really are, not just a number branded on a soul, but a self, a real self, exonerated of original sin. Consider the alternative. Consider a world gone mad. Imagine consciousness perverted. A government that invents the truth, an economy of people raised to graze designer identities. Consider not purgatory but Hell itself. The sins of man gone rampant. Things will grow hotter, will they not? There will be plagues? And disasters? Wars?"

The margins of the room gyrated. My mouth tasted like metal. I couldn't feel the scalpel in my hand.

"There are fish in the sea. Oil in the soil. Beasts in the wilds. What will we do with them? Will we plant the seed for future generations, or, given the chance, will we burn through God's harvest in a generation merely to satisfy our own desire, leaving nothing for the children of our children? Can you imagine a time when there won't be fish in the sea? Nor metal in the mountain? A time when beasts no longer roam the wilds?"

I was corrupted.

The Doctor's words rang true.

True to whom?

A madman such as me?

Was I mad?

Was I not mad, after all, for journeying to this place, of my own free will?

"And all for what? Original lust? Die before trying as a matter of trust, I see with staked hands a man before us who fixes and features and burrows a bribe, like a Pallas Athene, a winter-crossed bride."

"You reign down upon me a tirade of rhymes just to make me feel less than a bastard-bred child."

"You will cease and desist with rhetorical trysts. You are not all you wished that you were. You will bow before me, as a fief to a lord, and then become slave to my word."

"It is not for the Hare who despairs of the Fox as its searches for Pieces of Eight to resist what is missed between all that exists while only believing in fate."

"You will cease and desist..."

"You will cease to exist."

The Doctor dehisced.

"You will die like any other, collapsed beneath your House of Usher."

Lightning arrayed.

Sulfur swirled.

Feeling returned to my extremities.

The Doctor fumed.

"I abhor you."

"You abhor yourself."

"Ignorance is bliss. Time is an ever perfecting clockwork. What happens now will happen again."

"There is such a thing as free will."

"The stamp mark of original sin is free will."

"You lie."

"Would you be willing to decide your fate the instant you are born?"

"You are a liar."

"There's a daemon inside each one of us, just waiting to get out, a piece of hell inside us all, we'd rather do without. If I took you to a special place, a room fixed in the sky, and in the room one man was sane, the other'd gone awry, could you tell me which was which and numerate the reason why and ally with whom you then presume to have seen eye to eye?"

"If there is such a room, take me there."

The Doctor was malevolent.

"Open your eyes. We're already there. And the measure of your treasure, of your precious 'Pieces of Eight,' now lies within your own volition of a chance that came too late."

The Doctor's shadow emblazoned on the wall and I saw the figure in the hail, the reflection in the cooker, the thing at the ranch.

"It was you."

"The red box has allowed a breach. Nothing is beyond my reach."

"The black X and the pink circle…"

"For he whom time triggers, time is lost right from the start, for time gifts us naught but loss and a re-animated heart, which we try to piece together, but time winds on and on forever, for whatever we endeavor, soon begins to fall apart."

Rain hammered the casement. The glass case oscillated, the red box forked in black-bodied cavities, absorbing and re-radiating infinite wave forms.

"Consider the illusion of free will," the Doctor said. "Why does history repeat itself? If we know the past, we can change the future. So why, then, does the past rear its ugly head, over and over? It is *because* of the illusion of free will. You don't have to be religious to take a leap of faith."

"A leap of faith?"

I spotted my chance.

"Like the red box?"

"Yes," the Doctor agreed. "Like the red box."

"Show me. Show me the red box."

"Oh, I suppose I can let you take a look inside the looking glass. But don't blame me if you don't like what you see."

14 · The Red Box

The Doctor fit a skeleton key into the glass case.

"Ever wonder how ya' made it here?"

"Well I…"

"The institution is impenetrable. Everything's under lock and key. How did you get out of your cell? The exercise yard? And Menos Hall? The Bolgia?"

"I…"

"And the people you came across, how did they act?"

"I…"

"Did they act suspicious?"

"Well, they…"

"Or did they act like you weren't there?"

The Doctor picked up the red box.

I glommed the scalpel.

"What do you mean?"

The Doctor opened the balustrade door. Vertical nebulas rasterized the grayscale horizon.

A fir twisted in the wind.

"The Weeping Tree…"

The balustrade was ringed by a parapet. The Doctor set the red box on a plinth, looking over his shoulder.

"In the end, you and I are after the same thing, you know."

"What's that?"

"The reality behind the illusion."

"The illusion?"

"The illusion of free will. Life, as we know it, necessitates the absorption of other lives. By isolating the human soul I can sever the bonds of contrition."

"Would you experiment on yourself like you do on your victims?"

"Funny you should bring that up."

The balustrade was bowdlerized in mist, concealing all but the parapet, the Weeping Tree, and the red box.

The Doctor was exacerbating.

"But in order to begin the experiment, I'll need your help."

"Me?"

"Go ahead. Take a look."

Cloud droplets formed on my clothes.

The red box sat on the plinth.

It was irresistible.

"Open it."

I opened the red box.

I was blinded by something brilliant.

"Now do you see?"

A faded sun burned meekly.

"It's just a mirror."

"Look again."

The Doctor was right.

It wasn't a mirror.

Desire, drives, the mind, the soul, discordant facets of a whole began take a heavy toll upon a self I once extolled.

"Now do you see what you were all along?"

I could see the parts.

Mouth. Eyes. Ear. Hair.

The pieces held up.

But the whole wasn't there.

"Now do you see what we do all along, ignoring exactly the things that we long? Absolved of the curse of original sin you're digging a hole and you're filling it in."

I realized why people liked mirrors.

They yearned for a self; a whole.

But people were wrong.

There was no self.

There was no whole.

"You corrupt me…"

"With your own image?"

"I am forever corrupted!"

"By free will?"

I held my tongue.

"If it's free will you seek, in the mirror you must peek."

I disregarded the Doctor, a stranger to myself. I was not what I thought I was. Before, where I had been, were two discordant selves, two irreconcilable personalities, each with its own aspect, a perfect, mirror image of who I wanted to be and what I had instead become, a series of epistemological contingencies one would mistake as having a life.

The cathexis was brilliant.

It was all that I wanted.

The Doctor put his hand on my shoulder.

"Now do you see why I gift them this gift? To be rid of this ruse? This ill designed queue? Serving the servile, august and deranged, picking apart the delirious brain?"

I tired of the Doctor.

All I wanted was the red box.

"One question remains," the Doctor complained.

"What's that?"

"You."

"Me?"

"Who told you where I was?"

"Andrews."

"Andrews? No, no….."

"Well," I stammered, "when I moved into the House I…"

"You went to the House," the Doctor exclaimed, "to the one place you weren't supposed to go?"

"What do you mean 'weren't supposed to go?' As if you owned me."

"Stop. You'll have to go back. We'll try it again. Believe me, Andrews will wish he was never born. Hey, stop! Don't look in the mirror! Don't you know what you're risking? I tell you, you've got to stop! Don't you get it? You can still go back. It's not too late. Don't you want to go back? You must go back, you must, because, if you don't, if you don't..."

"What could be worse than this madhouse?"

"You don't understand…"

"What?"

"It is not what you think. You'll see yourself as you really are."

I couldn't take my eyes off myself.

"What have you done? What have you done? It's too late. It's too late. I can see it on your face. You're beginning to piece it together. Yes? I put the knife and the poker in the dumbwaiter. I hid the pieces in the attic. Then I mopped the floor. But it doesn't matter. No matter how hard I try, the pieces never fit together. But you know all about that. You were there! You saw the whole thing."

The Weeping Tree torqued. The spinning wheel spun in reverse. A jewel shone atop a ladder of thorns. A stone was cast. A hole was dug. A sign was hung. The Mephistophelean House was for rent.

I reached out.

Behind my shoulder I could see the Doctor.

"Don't you realize what the things in the basement are?"

"The things with flies for eyes?"

And it was then, as I looked in the mirror, I saw there was only one person on the balcony, and that I was talking to myself.